WAR DANCER

Deborah Best Baney

Cover Design by Leo Sapik
Cover Artwork by Shannon L. Simmermon
Cover Graphic Design by Visual Image Design,
Debby Brust
Back Cover Graphics by Visual Image Design,
Debby Brust

ISBN #978-0-615-40062-4 ISBN-13-Paper

www.wardancernovel.com

I

Dedication

To: Michael Roderick Baney,
my knight in shining armour!

Acknowledgements

First and foremost, I wish to thank my "Ghost Writer" Lord Perazim, for giving me a story to write and then teaching me how to write it. He also brought others to come alongside me to help in my first effort.

I want to thank my husband, Michael. You not only encouraged me, you also helped me set scenes and are quite the creative genius when I hit writer's block. I look forward to the fun of working together on the sequel!

Thank you, Lori Sloderbech, for working with me in the editing process. You took my story and made it into a book. I learned a lot from you and am blessed to have you for my friend!

I also want to acknowledge Lori's son, Cole Moreland for offering fantastic suggestions and making such insightful observations. You have a bright future ahead of you as a writer!

It is a real pleasure working with Debby Brust and Shannon Simmermon. Again, Lord Perazim brought us together for this project and in the process, we have become friends.

Great job, "Sir Leo the Dragonslayer" Sapik, for designing the artwork on the cover!

Thank you, Leo and Becky Sapik; what friends you have been to Michael and me for 15 years! Your input and encouragement mean so much - not to mention how grateful we are to Lord Perazim for bringing us together as the "Us 4 and No More Warriors." (No one else wanted to join us at 5:30am Monday through Friday!)

I must express my gratitude to "Sister Mary Elizabeth," my mother, Mary Best. You read through the manuscript one final time with me. Your knack for "nit-picking" proved to be a valuable attribute!
It has been many years – sixth grade I believe, since you helped me with a major project (flags of the world) – I am grateful to have your diligent help again with this project! We shared some great laughs together, too. Thanks, mom!

I wish to acknowledge the loving memory of my father, Donald Best, aka "Bishop Donald."

Though he did not have the pleasure of being involved with this project, he does have the joy, being a part of that great cloud of witnesses of watching me do what he longed to do, write a book. I know that he is proud of his "darling daughter Debbie."

VI

Contents

Dedication   I

Acknowledgements   II

Prologue   V

Chapter   **Page**

1 The Invisible Army   1

2 Putting on the Whole Armour   6

3 Worship Warrior   17

4 Disguise of the Asmodai   22

5 Knighthood   29
    Day 1: Feasting and Discourse
       Apprentice-Knight of Prayer   39
    Day 2: Knighting Ceremony   45
    Day 3: The Tournament!   51

6 The Hunt   60

7 The Prank   70

8 Captured by the Asmodai   80

9 Into the Caverns of Cataclysmic Calamities   89

10 The Dark and Stormy Night   103

11 Stay at the Abbey   113
     The Tale   119

12 Bamboozled!   129

13 Battle at Brookshire   142

14 Brighton Castle   148

15 Garrett's Dream   161

16 Celebration Day   173

17 Supernatural Weapons   186

18 Setting the Stage for War   199
     Asmo's Plot
     Preparing for War   202

19 Skirmishes   207

20 Attacked!   213
     Staging
     Warfare   218

21 Captured!   227

Prologue

In a land before time and space there lived a King. A good and wise Ruler who created all that is. He loved beauty of every kind, so whatever the Sovereign made brought him great joy because of its splendor.

The King used exquisite gemstones more brilliant than any rainbow to build his castle. Then he filled his kingdom with an overflowing variety of flowers, trees and animals. Finally, the Monarch created a host of magnificent celestial spirits, his servants. The king loved music so much that he created a special spirit with internal organs that resounded with glorious music throughout the entire palace whenever he moved.

His Royal Majesty's name was Elyon. He had a son, His Royal Highness, Prince Sabaoth, commander over all the celestial spirits.

In his court, King Elyon's trusted confidant and advisor, the Lord High Chancellor, Lord Perazim, likewise did the sovereign's bidding.

Asmo, the beloved minstrel of the high court, also ruled over one third of the celestial spirits. King Elyon delighted in the presence of

Asmo because his music caused the Supreme Ruler to dance and sing.

One day, King Elyon called a counsel with Prince Sabaoth and Lord Perazim. "I have decided to create another world," The Sovereign began.

Prince Sabaoth and Lord Perazim smiled at each other, knowingly. Everything King Elyon created turned out well and the process always involved a great deal of enjoyment!

The Monarch continued, "I want to create a world that is only temporary and confined to limitations I call time and space."

"Go on," encouraged Prince Sabaoth.

"I must first construct a universe and solar systems within it to support life on the planet where I wish to make my new creation," His Majesty said, smiling with eager enthusiasm at His new project.

"What kind of new creation?" asked Lord Perazim.

"A mortal creation," answered the King.

Bewildered, the Prince looked over at the Chancellor, who returned the same expression.

King Elyon resumed, "I desire to make this new planet to be a shadow of my kingdom. I want my special creation to rule over it and to make it flourish. Like my kingdom here, there will be an abundance of plant life and beautiful

minerals and species of animals." With a gleam of delight, the Royal Creator stopped momentarily to give extra emphasis to his next statement. "What will separate my mortals from the rest of that world is I shall breathe into them my breath of life. Unlike the plants and animals that they will care for, my new creation will have an immortal soul," said the Sovereign. "I will assign my servants to watch over them; and Lord Perazim, you will bring answers, guidance and comfort to my mortals when they are in need.
We shall be invisible to them, but they shall know us through different means outside their mortal senses," King Elyon finished with a laugh of joy.

"If the mortals will have an immortal soul, then why make this new world merely temporary?" asked the Prince.

"I have timeless plans in mind for these creatures who at first will be bound to time," smiled the king.

The king, his son and advisor worked out every detail together. From out of nowhere an entire universe filled with stars and planets and moons appeared. Now all was in place to sustain the planet made especially for this new creation called Mortal.

Asmo, in the meantime, continued to govern over his third of the Great Sovereign's realm, as he had done since his own creation.

XI

However, something began to change. New thoughts emerged in the spirit's mind, and he took heed of them.

"*I am the most beautiful of all King Elyon's celestial beings,*" Asmo said to himself. "*I am wise and respected by all the hosts of the realm. Why am I beneath the King? I should be equal with Him!*"

Suddenly, the music resonating from his internal instruments jarred a discordant note. Asmo took his legions of spirits and rose up against the Monarch. Prince Sabaoth, along with his other two generals waged war against Asmo and his traitors.

After the Great Cosmic War, Prince Sabaoth threw Asmo and his minions from his Father's realm. As they hurtled like lightning from King Elyon's empire, they fell into the universe of time and space. Their splendor transformed to become grotesque and hideous. Asmo's musical instruments shattered. Now whenever the sounds of joy for King Elyon resonated against his ruined organs he experienced intolerable excruciating pain.

With all the intense hatred and wounded pride in his evil heart, Asmo plotted and schemed until he found a crafty way to settle the score with King Elyon. He would steal away the love of mortals for their Creator.

In the fullness of time, King Elyon sent Prince Sabaoth into the new planet to win them back. The only way for the Prince to win was to die. His flawless blood freed every mortal throughout all time who chose to love their invisible Creator again.

Asmo thought he had finally become victorious over King Elyon by slaying his only son; but to his great horror, the Prince not only came back to life, he also bestowed upon those who fight for King Elyon the same supernatural powers he has to fight against Asmo and his asmodai minions.

Asmo has a new battle to wage: to render mortals with supernatural powers captive and defenseless. Among his primary targets: the spiritual war dancer.

XIII

XIV

The Invisible Enemy

Chapter 1

He ran so fast he thought his lungs would burst. Panic made him glance behind as he fled into the ancient forest. The warm morning sunlight barely penetrated the dense leafy canopy making the stand of old gnarled trees very dark and cool. As the tall trees closed in behind him, Garrett slowed his pace to a brisk walk to avoid stumbling over the tangled undergrowth and fallen trunks decaying on the soft ground. Although the filtered rays of the sun streaming through the thick foliage helped Garrett see his way, nothing could help him see the foe chasing after him. One thing Garrett knew for sure, there were a lot of them and the obstacles and darkness of the woods did not hinder them at all the way it did him!

The strange shadows and darting images Garrett saw just out of the corners of his eyes seemed to vanish when he looked straight at them. He could not detect anything with his natural senses, only the palpable fear which he could almost taste. Panting for every breath, Garrett felt the blood drain from his face as exhaustion began to overtake him. He couldn't go on....but he had to – his life depended on it! The young lad found himself tripping on the twisting vines in the underbrush.

Catching his foot on a rock camouflaged in the leafy undergrowth, Garrett tumbled forward. He let out a terrified gasp when in that same instant invisible hands fiercely grabbed him from behind and forcefully yanked him back up. No matter which way Garrett turned or tried to move, he could not leave the spot where he stood. An invisible barrier kept him trapped as if confined in a glass cage. He sensed his enemy gleefully celebrating the capture of one of King Elyon's subjects. He knew that when his captors finished their revelry, they would take him away with them down to the Caverns of Cataclysmic Calamity. Once a prisoner there, escape became nearly impossible. Few had succeeded in getting out, and he'd heard about their tortures and terrible agonies. Rumours even suggested that fire-breathing dragons kept their lairs in the caverns!

Garrett's thoughts began to become clear again as he regained his breath and the throbbing pulse in his temples slowed. Fear somehow subsided, renewing his ability to remember the strategies he had learned during warfare training. Any possibility of escape would require using the proper tactics against the unseen foe. Sir Roderick, the lord of Bane Manor, oversaw the training of Garrett along with the other pages and squires.

Garrett remembered the lectures that Sir Roderick gave them. *"Know your enemy,"* instructed the knight. *"There are two kinds of foes in this world: mortal and immortal. It is imperative to know which weapon to use and the proper strategy for the kind of battle you will fight. You fight your mortal enemy with the sword and the lance, and you fight the immortal asmodai with your mind and your spirit."*

The celebration that Garrett perceived going on in the invisible world became audible. As the hideous sounds swelled around him, Garrett worked hard to remember what he should do to break free. *"Bring to your mind the lessons that are going deep into your spirit,"* he heard Sir Roderick admonish.

"Which lessons?!" Garrett cried out in anguish. Just then, Lord Perazim brought to the lad's mind the singing and dancing they did at St. Rebecca's during chapel.

"What does THIS have to do with anything?" he often wondered until he learned that the asmodai could not hold him when he sang and

danced before Prince Sabaoth. The tremor of the music and worship in the dance grated against their being so much, it felt like torture to the asmodai; they had no choice but to flee away.

Garrett calmed himself, quietly regulating his breathing for a moment. Then with a deep breath he let out a strong loud sound.

"Prince Sabaoth!
You are the Lord of Hosts!
Before You,
No enemy can boast.
Hallelu-jah, hallelujah!"

All the shadows and movement stopped. The hideous sounds ceased. Garrett still felt their presence, but he could move now. Doing the simple dance of a spiritual war dancer, Garrett rapidly clapped his hands, stomped his feet, turned half way round then back again. Raising his hands above his head, he then bent at the waist while skipping in a circle, all the while singing.

So caught up in his dance, Garrett forgot about the presence of the enemy. Eventually, Garrett became aware that they had fled just the way Sir Roderick said.

"I have just won my first battle!" Garrett laughed out loud with gladness at his victory against the asmodai.

Garrett did not feel alone in the dark forest; he felt the presence of joy and the pleasure of his invisible Sovereign.

Continuing deeper into the woods, the young lad began to realize that until he arrived safely inside the castle walls of Bane Manor; his only real safety was to resume his songs of tribute to Prince Sabaoth. As Garrett made his way steadily through the tangles of underbrush, he sang the happiest songs he had learned from chapel services.

Before long, Garrett found himself on the other side of the forest. Leaving the gloomy and foreboding woods behind, the lad stepped out into the glorious sunshine and grassy meadow once more. His heart filled with joy as he began to understand Sir Roderick's hearty laughter.

Garrett ran all the way back up to the manor, eager for the opportunity to tell Sir Roderick about his victory. *"My lord will be pleased to learn of my first battle* and *my first victory!"* the page thought to himself. *"I am not even a squire yet and already I know the thrill of victory!"*

High in the celestial realm, King Elyon could not contain his delight at young Garrett's victory; He jumped up and danced with Prince Sabaoth around his throne.

Putting on the Whole Armour

Chapter 2

𝔅reathless and utterly exhausted Garrett reached the manor gate. The savory aromas wafting throughout the courtyard increased the youth's already ravenous appetite as he headed toward the kitchen for some water. Dinner, as the noon meal was called, would not be ready for another hour.

Coming upon the busy activities of the kitchen, Garrett observed Janie the head cook, instructing a helper on how to prepare the wild game Sir Roderick had brought in from his hunt. Seeing that Janie and her helper were preoccupied, Garrett slipped a freshly baked roll in his tunic.

"Don't be stealing food off the lord's table before it is even served him, young page!" scolded Janie.

But noticing his flushed face softened her rebuke. Janie's helper put down her carving knife and wiped her hands on her apron while fetching a tall glass of water for Garrett. Acknowledging her, he sat down on a wooden stool to take a long drink and eat his roll.

"What have you been doing this bright, cheerful morn that you should be so spent?" Janie asked with curiosity.

Not wishing to tell his story to everyone, Garrett simply replied, "Running." With that, he waved farewell and headed over to the chapel to see Bishop Donald.

Since Garrett knew he could not speak with Sir Roderick until after his training session later that afternoon and he needed to tell *someone,* he chose the bishop. As the minister of Bane Manor and overseer of the clergy in the surrounding villages under Lord Roderick's domain, Bishop Donald gave wise counsel, watched out for everyone and gained the confidence of all as a trusted advisor.

The bishop sat in concentrated thought at his desk. The sound of quickly approaching footsteps echoing on the stone floor interrupted his musings. He recognized Garrett's youthful stride and the bishop always welcomed Garrett's intrusions upon his contemplations.

Garrett arrived at the open door and rapped lightly. Putting his thoughts aside as he leaned back in his chair, Bishop Donald gave his full attention to the lad and motioned for him to sit down.

As Garrett settled himself into the chair, he exuberantly began his story. "I left the manor early this morning to practice hunting with my bow and arrow. I found the perfect spot on the other side of the trees jutting out from the main forest. Just as I shot my last arrow at a gray rabbit," Garrett went on, "I suddenly felt the invisible army surrounding me. I dropped my bow and ran into the woods. I was scared."

Bishop Donald listened in fascination to Garrett's story and thought to himself. *"Not many people I know have actually encountered the invisible enemy so directly."*

"Then the asmodai captured me!" Garrett said. "That was even more frightening! But Lord Perazim reminded me of the lessons Sir Roderick taught us and also for me to do my dance the way you taught in chapel. Pretty soon the asmodai fled and I was free," the young page said with elation as he finished his brief summary of the encounter.

"Garrett," the bishop said, "your story is very intriguing because the asmodai usually hide themselves in or around a mortal. They cleverly insinuate themselves into a person's thoughts in order to inflict harmful emotions on them such as fear, discouragement, anger, and even confusion so that one would think they were fighting against another mortal and choose the wrong weapons," explained the bishop.

Affirming Garrett's progress with his spiritual weaponry, Bishop Donald said encouragingly, "I am happy to see that you are taking to heart the lessons taught you by Sir Roderick, Lady Isabelle and myself."

Leaning closer to impress the seriousness upon him, Bishop Donald went on. "These are perilous times we live in, Garrett. The asmodai are now using many different tactics with which to attack us. The enemy has even succeeded in deceiving some mortals with their magickal powers so much so that they worship these evil spirits. However, when a mortal knows what his weapons are and how to use them, that mortal becomes a spiritual warrior more powerful than Asmo. Those mortals that the asmodai have deceived do not know that Asmo's power is no match for the power and authority of Prince Sabaoth!"

Before the bishop could continue, the sound of the dinner bell ringing reminded Garrett that the roll he had snatched earlier merely took the edge off his hunger for a short while. The kind bishop told Garrett on the way to the great hall that he would be most glad to look for his lost bow after dinner.

"It would not go well for you to lose any piece of weaponry – especially when you are soon to become a squire!"

Coming into the great hall, the smell of the game that Janie and her helper had prepared that morning filled the room with its savoury aroma. In spite of his hunger, Garrett and the other pages served the rest of the household before they and the kitchen staff ate. As the household from all over the manor arrived to sit, Garrett and the other pages brought the platters and pitchers from the kitchen to the table.

Sir Roderick and Lady Isabelle sat at opposite ends of the long table. The lesser knights, squires and ladies-in-waiting filled the benches on either side.

Finally when the pages sat for their own meal, Garrett leaned over to his friend, Sekiah. "Meet me after practice this afternoon. I have something important to tell you!"

After dinner, Sir Roderick along with several of the squires, who assisted the knight in training, went to the practice field to work with the pages on their sword play. Garrett used a blunt wooden sword and small round shield called a buckler, just as all the pages did; but he knew that he was ready to use a real sword. He could hardly wait for the day Sir Roderick would make him a squire! *"Now that I have fought the asmodai and won, I know I can face mortals in combat, too!"* Garrett thought to himself.

Sir Roderick informed the older pages they would begin their first lance practice.

"Garrett," Sir Roderick directed, "You go first."

Calming his excitement, Garrett mounted a chestnut Rouncey, a lightweight war horse used by the squires. Grabbing the lance a squire handed him, he held it poised to strike the quintain, a shield suspended from a swinging pole with a sandbag attached to the other end of the crossbar. Focusing his attention straight ahead, Garrett charged. Confidence from the morning's victory surged through the page giving him a feeling of superb strength and agility.

While the others cheered him on, Garrett struck the apparatus with a great THUD! Making it spin wildly, he could not maneuver himself away fast enough to miss the sandbag from smacking him on the back of the head. Losing his balance, he went plunging from his steed as his lance went crashing to the ground. The hilarious spectacle caused a great deal of laughter among the pages and squires watching!

"Good show!" chuckled Spencer, one of Sir Roderick's squires. "I thought Sir Roderick had you go first so the other pages could see how it's supposed to be done!"

"Hey Garrett, good thing that dummy didn't have a lance to fight back with or you would suffer more than just wounded pride!" teased Tyler, another squire.

Gathering himself up and retrieving his lance, Garrett passed it off to another of the older pages. The lad felt a bit chagrined that his mortal readiness did not yet match his spiritual warfare abilities. However, shaking it off, Garrett enjoyed the amusing laughter and poking fun at the other pages as they went for their first try at it!

"Just because you and Spencer are nearing knighthood," Sir Roderick said to Tyler, "does not mean you should be so cocky. I still remember when the two of you gave your first try!" he said with a twinkle in his eye.

"Ah," replied Tyler. "The only advantage you have over any of us, my liege, is that we were not present to witness your first attempt at jousting the quintain!"

"Tis true, squire," Sir Roderick smiled. "I can say I was proficient in all the armaments from my very first try!"

"Oh!" laughed Tyler. "None of us would believe you without proof!"

"Very well," allowed the knight. "I did indeed have my share of falls."

Practice finally came to an end and everyone took their turn dipping a ladleful of water from the wooden bucket to refresh themselves before sitting down on the ground to relax. This gave Sir Roderick the opportunity to work with his pages' further instruction on their spiritual weapons.

Garrett breathed a sigh of relief, knowing he would not have to bide his time much longer. *"I will soon be able to tell Sir Roderick of the battle I had this morning,"* the page said to himself.

"I am preparing you to fight in warfare," Sir Roderick began, "because we never know when we will be attacked by an enemy, seen or unseen."

Garrett's heart leapt at these words, since now he had indeed experienced the truth of them.

"Vikings have attacked far off castles in Britanniae," continued the lord. "Reports are that they may be heading toward us. Therefore, we must be ready. I am also making you ready to fight Asmo and his minions. So now we will work on becoming more familiar with our spiritual armour," said the knight. "Which one of you can name all the weapons and armour in your spiritual arsenal?" the lord asked, as he looked intently at each of his squires and pages.

As the pages settled down to gather their thoughts for the answer, Sir Roderick called upon

Garrett to recite the list. Garrett spoke up with a steady voice, speaking as though he actually went through the motions of suiting up his mortal body. "Buckle on the belt of Truth around your waist. Put on the breastplate of Righteousness. Lace on the shoes of readiness to proclaim the good news of Peace; take up the shield of Faith, which is Trust, to put out all the flaming arrows of the invisible enemy. Wear the helmet of Deliverance and wield the sword that Lord Perazim provides, which is the Sacred Scroll from our King Elyon. Send messages to King Elyon at all times of all kinds, including requests, using the Secret Language from Lord Perazim, being always vigilant and persistent on behalf of all the King's subjects."

Delighted with the progress of his page, Sir Roderick noticed the look of confidence on Garrett's countenance. *"Could it be the young page has actually used some of these spiritual weapons?"* the knight wondered.

"That's enough for the day," Sir Roderick announced to the weary soldiers–in–training. "Come prepared next time to tell me the use of each piece of armour." Sir Roderick rose while the rest noisily shuffled out into the courtyard.

Finding his opportunity at last, Garrett approached the knight and asked, "Sir Roderick, something happened to me this morning and I used one of the spiritual weapons. May I tell you about it?"

"You certainly may, Garrett," Sir Roderick answered with interest motioning for them to move over to a quiet corner where they could talk undisturbed.

When the page finished telling the knight his story, Sir Roderick commended Garrett: "That's quite impressive, Garrett! An encounter with the asmodai can be intimidating and you showed great fortitude in your first confrontation. Not only that, but the weapon you used is not even in the list you just quoted. Most mortals do not even know that praise is a weapon."

"I remember Bishop Donald preaching about it one time," replied Garrett. "He said that expressing admiration to Prince Sabaoth for his character and abilities is one of the most powerful weapons in our arsenal.'"

"I am pleased with your progress, Garrett," said Sir Roderick. "I can see that you have the makings of becoming a great knight."

"Sir Roderick, I think I know why you have so much confidence," stated Garrett.

"Oh?" Sir Roderick said.

"It's because of the many battles you have won against the asmodai. You are not afraid of anything," explained the page.

"Well," replied the veteran warrior, "that is part of it, to be sure. But the other part is the trust I have in our Great King Elyon. My confidence comes from him, not in my own abilities. We have to have abilities in order to fight; we just need to remember who gives us the strength and courage to do it. Now when you can hit the quintain without getting smacked, I'll know just what kind of mortal warrior you will become!" Sir Roderick said laughing.

"I hope to be just as good at fighting mortals as immortals," Garrett said.

"No doubt someday you will be," the knight replied.

With that, Garrett left the practice field and briskly walked through the courtyard looking for his friend.

Worship Warrior

Chapter 3

Sekiah dashed through the courtyard, darting this way and that to avoid the knights and squires sparring with each other. Young children chased around the harried servants bustling about in the late afternoon finishing up the days' chores. Garrett met Sekiah and the two made their way back through the courtyard with lightness in their steps.

"Let's hurry, Garrett," Sekiah said eagerly. "I have lots to tell you about my lessons with Lady Isabelle this afternoon."

Instead of training with the other pages and squires on this particular day, Sekiah went to his music and banner lessons after dinner. When the long afternoon ended, he rushed to the freedom that awaited.

Lady Isabelle Bane taught all the pages religion, music, dance, and manners, as well as how to read and write. Devoted to the Holy Scriptures themselves, Lord and Lady Bane believed it their duty to educate the pages while in training at the castle so they too could read the

Holy Scroll and also the great works of religious scholars.

Lady Isabelle took note of the unique talents that Sekiah demonstrated in music. He could already play several instruments well and sang with a strong, clear voice. But more than that, Sekiah possessed an ability to bring others into worship to Great King Elyon. The lady worked diligently with Sekiah to perfect his skill with this special weapon.

Worship warriors not only went into battle with the other knights, they led the way in front of the rest of the soldiers. This meant that his training became specialized. The worship warrior led the troops with songs and chants, and also carried banners when riding into battle. He must know which flag to wave because each color symbolized the kind of conflict they entered. Sometimes it was used as a signal for help from a neighboring fortress.

Making sure no one saw them, the pages walked quickly past the kitchen on their way to the great hall. Garrett and Sekiah stealthily made their way over to the secret passageway located behind the large tapestry hanging on the wall near the fireplace. For use in times of sieges, the passageway led through a tunnel to a distance outside the castle so the inhabitants could either escape or bring in fresh supplies and reinforcements during a blockade. Sekiah lit the candle he brought to see with in the darkness as the boys hurried toward the freedom of the orchards where the passageway took them.

Sekiah blew out the candle and laid it near the opening along with the pouch of flint and steel. The lads ran to their favourite tree and climbed up into the lower branches. Situating themselves, the evening breeze cooled the youths as it rustled through the leaves.

Sekiah told Garrett how Asmo hated the worship warriors more than any of the knights because they incited the other soldiers to praise when going into battle which always brought defeat to the asmodai.

"Does that make you nervous to become a worship warrior?" Garrett asked, intrigued.

"No," Sekiah stated matter of factly. "I *want* to fight Asmo and his asmodai underlings! Besides the songs for war, Lady Isabelle is teaching me songs for deliverance, healing and victory," Sekiah resumed. "Each kind of song has a banner and even a dance."

When Sekiah finished elaborating on the banners, Garrett told Sekiah about the incident in the woods that had taken place that very same morning. How the asmodai had run away after capturing him when he sang and danced the spiritual war dance to Prince Sabaoth.

Though impressed with his friend's victory, Sekiah struggled with jealousy. *"After all, I'm the one receiving the special training in worship and warfare against the asmodai, so I should be the one to have the first victory, not Garrett!"* Sekiah said to himself.

The mood changed between the boys. Garrett detected a vague feeling of distance develop between himself and Sekiah, but passed it off.

Twilight turned the sky into beautiful shades of pink and purple; but in the orchard, the quickly descending nightfall alerted the pages to the sense of urgency of returning to the manor. Suppertime approached, and Janie expected the lads on time to serve.

"We must hurry back," Garrett said, slightly agitated. "Janie will be harsh with us if we are not on time!"

Running back, neither boy said anything. Garrett reached the entrance first and grabbed the pouch. Sekiah held the candle as Garrett lit it using the flint and steel. Coming toward the end of the tunnel, Sekiah blew out the candle and darted ahead of Garrett. Sekiah caught him off guard by hurrying out of the tunnel before Garrett could catch up, leaving him to grope his way in the blackness. By the time Garrett came to the end of the passageway, Sekiah had disappeared.

"What is bothering Sekiah?" Garrett wondered to himself. "He's peeved about something, but why take it out on me!"

Peering out from behind the tapestry, Garrett made sure that no one in the grand hall would see where he had emerged. A couple of younger pages with their backs to the wall chatted with each other as they set the table. Walking quickly but trying to appear nonchalant, Garrett passed through the grand hall unnoticed. Coming into the kitchen Garrett found Sekiah already helping Janie get the platters ready to serve the household their supper. Janie kept the boys busy which made it easy for them to steer clear of each other.

At last they sat down to their own meal along with the other pages and kitchen staff. Bitterness made Sekiah nearly too angry to eat. Garrett felt bewildered and reacted in annoyance to his friend's strange attitude.

Finally the day came to an end. Both lads fell exhausted and angry into their beds.

Disguise of the Asmodai

Chapter 4

Morning dawned cold. Soft shades of gray and blue illuminated the crisp clear sky revealing the occasional wispy cloud gently drifting by. With a blast, a guard trumpeted the day's start. The sun not yet risen above the horizon provided scant light to the servants already up, scurrying about stoking the fires in the kitchen and great hall. Preparations for the simple morning meal were underway.

After breakfast, everyone at Bane Manor gathered in St. Rebecca's Chapel behind the courtyard for a short devotional. Standing in front of the pulpit in a more casual way than during the formal Sunday service, Bishop Donald gave a brief message, and then he prayed.

This morning, the topic concerned putting aside offenses. As he proceeded to elaborate, Bishop Donald noticed out of the corner of his eyes two pages shifting uncomfortably where they stood.

"It matters not what another has done to you," the bishop began. "What matters is your own response. By holding onto the offense, you lock the shackles around your own heart that holds you to the anger or resentment caused by the deed of that mortal. Unlock it! Let it go! Free yourself from the grievance that keeps you in chains," the bishop implored. "If not, you will become bitter and bitterness is a poison that will kill your heart. One day you will find that it has consumed your personality and you are no longer your true self!"

Garrett and Sekiah glanced down at the ground. Yesterday they were best friends, but now they held a grudge against each other. Bishop Donald asked Lord Perazim to give each person the desire to forgive anyone who had hurt them.

As the little congregation left to resume their duties, Bishop Donald beckoned Garrett and Sekiah to come over. Reluctantly they obeyed following the chaplain into his study.

"I see that my message made you lads uncomfortable this morning," he began. "Do either of you want to tell me the offense that has come between the two of you?"

Waiting on their slow response the chaplain thought about how he could help the youths standing before him once again value their friendship.

"'Tis a shame to see two life-long friends quarrel over something that I am certain can easily be worked out. You fellas came here eight years ago as little lads. Your fathers each brought you to this manor at the same time to train under Lord Roderick." Bishop Donald said this to remind the youths of their enduring friendship in order to help them gain perspective of the rift between them.

"I saw you two on the day of your arrival," the chaplain continued. "You were each scared when your fathers left you here and went back to their estates. But you soon became friends and until now, have remained true to each other. Is the offense you are feeling right now greater than all the years of your friendship?"

Sekiah studied the tops of his shoes, ashamed of his jealousy. Garrett looked at Sekiah, but couldn't think of any reason for his friend's sudden hateful attitude toward him. Finally, Sekiah spoke up.

"It's not fair that Garrett got to fight the asmodai first!" He said with scorn. "I'm the one in training to fight against the invisible enemy. Garrett is learning to fight against mortals so I should have the first battle!"

Garrett felt his face turn red with anger. "I'll fight against you, mortal!" He said infuriated as he lunged toward Sekiah with clenched fists.

Bishop Donald stepped between the two pages before a fight could break out. "Garrett," the bishop said, his voice firm with authority. "Can you ask Prince Sabaoth to help you forgive Sekiah for taking his resentment out on you?" he asked.

Garrett, taken aback that the bishop would speak to him first shifted uncomfortably as he looked around. "Why are you asking me?" he stated defiantly. "After all, Sekiah started this!"

"You are just as much at fault in this quarrel because of your own attitude," replied the bishop. "How about asking Prince Sabaoth to restore the right spirit within you so you can forgive Sekiah?"

"I'll try," Garrett said grudgingly. Garrett said what he felt in his heart. "Prince Sabaoth, I hate Sekiah."

"Try it again, Garrett," prodded Bishop Donald.

"Prince Sabaoth, can you forgive Sekiah for me? I hate him and I can't."

"Again," said the bishop.

"Prince Sabaoth, can I hit him real hard just once? Then maybe I could forgive him. Okay, I'll pray better this time," Garrett quickly added before Bishop Donald could correct him once more.

Garrett looked down at the floor while taking several deep breaths which helped him to focus on what he needed to say. Then closing his eyes Garrett said, "Prince Sabaoth, I can't forgive Sekiah and I really don't want to. But I do know that if I don't, I won't be able to become a knight, and I really want to be a knight someday. Please help me to forgive Sekiah."

"Now that was honest, Garrett. When you speak that way - truly from your heart, Prince Sabaoth will help you to talk to him in even better ways for Sekiah's sake. This will help you to become the knight you wish to be," Bishop Donald said.

Sekiah stood by shamefacedly while his friend worked on forgiving him. Staring at the floor, Sekiah could not look at Garrett because he knew his jealousy had brought this all on them.

Now the bishop turned to Sekiah. "Do you realize that the asmodai attacked you while Garrett was telling you about his victory and you fell right into their trap?"

Shocked to hear this, Sekiah jerked his head up. "I was attacked? What trap?" he asked in dismay. He should know the answer, but he could not think of it.

"One of the ways the asmodai attacks us is through our emotions. The weapon that got you is called 'Jealousy,'" answered the bishop.

"Oh, yes," sighed Sekiah. "I really blew it. Bishop Donald, how can I be a worship warrior if I get jealous of other people doing things that I think I should get to do first?"

"That is a good question," Bishop Donald replied. "Pretend you are Garrett and you come and tell Sekiah what just happened to you. How would you want Sekiah to react?"

"I would want Sekiah to be glad that I, I mean Garrett, made it out of the forest and not be taken down to the Caverns of Cataclysmic Calamities."

"Are you glad, Sekiah?" Bishop Donald asked earnestly.

For an answer, Sekiah looked over at Garrett and said, "I won't be jealous of you anymore, Garrett. I *am* glad that you got away from the terrible asmodai!"

Bishop Donald made one last statement to the boys. "You have just used another weapon in your arsenal, fellas." Sekiah and Garrett looked at each other in bewilderment. The bishop continued: "It is forgiveness. Anytime we ask for forgiveness, we humble ourselves and Asmo is defeated. It was pride that got him thrown out of the celestial city. Humility is the opposite of pride and our first weapon in winning any battle!"

Garrett and Sekiah left the chaplain and headed toward the great hall. Excitement hung in the air as the many preparations for the grand celebration ahead caused a great deal of commotion.

Knighthood:

Day 1
Feasting and Discourse

Chapter 5

The day had finally come! Now began the three days of ceremony and festivities in the final stage of the squire's transition from boyhood to manhood and from commoner to royalty. Sir Roderick would dub two of his squires to knighthood. The time had also arrived for Garrett and Sekiah to move into the next stage of their training by becoming squires.

There would be much feasting and in depth discussions with royals and other nobility along with members of the clergy who had come to participate in this marked occasion. The topics of conversation centered on the roles and responsibilities of a knight.

Garrett and Sekiah took every opportunity to listen and observe while helping Janie set the heavy platters on the long wooden tables and carry out other numerous chores of serving. The tables covered with white linen cloths were filled with a variety of delicacies.

Sekiah took notice as an impressive-looking guest seized the attention of one of the squires.

"Spencer," the noble said in a strong, authoritative voice, "I am known as Sir Leo the Dragon-Slayer. Lord Roderick and I fought together many a time. We trained under King Waymon."

"I have heard much about you from my liege," Spencer replied. "I am delighted to meet you at last!" he stated with enthusiasm. "He loves to regale us with the tales of his glory days with you."

"'His glory days!'" guffawed the knight. "His may be over, but mine are most certainly not!" Sir Leo laughed with amusement. "I am here to see just how well he has trained his new protégée. So let me ask you, what is the most important weapon of a knight and why?"

"Well, your lordship," Spencer responded with assurance. "My most important weapon is my shield. It will protect me from the attacks of any enemy. My spiritual shield is my Faith. Without it, none of my other weapons have any value. Even the sword of Truth will not pierce the enemy if I do not have faith to believe in the power of Prince Sabaoth, who fought the ultimate battle for me."

"Well stated!" replied the noble, "I do believe that your training under Lord Roderick has proven to be most profitable. Now the test comes in the field of battle. It is one thing to know this in your head, quite another when the enemy is before you."

Having just set a water pitcher on the table, Garrett overheard an earl question the other apprentice knight. He lingered to hear the response.

"Tyler," asked the earl, "After putting on your spiritual armour what is your next task?"

Without hesitation Tyler answered, "I wait to receive instructions from Lord Perazim."

"Good answer," the earl said thoughtfully. Continuing on with his examination of the youth's education of knighthood, the earl challenged the apprentice knight with another test of his knowledge. "In the fourteenth century, The Duke of Burgandy describes the virtues in the Knight's Code of Chivalry that all knights are to demonstrate. Can you name them for me?"

"There are twelve virtues, your lordship," Tyler began, "Faith, Charity, Justice, Sagacity, Prudence, Temperance, Resolution, Truth, Liberality, Diligence, Hope and Valour."

"Excellent," the earl replied enthusiastic- ally. "Explain to me the meaning of each one."

"Very well, your lordship," answered Tyler. "It is always helpful to recite the 12 virtues so that the rehearsing of them makes the merit of each go deeper into one's soul.

"Faith," the candidate began, "means to trust in King Elyon. Charity means to love all mortals through practical demonstrations."

"Such as?" the earl inquired.

"Providing aide to those in need, particularly destitute widows and orphans," answered the squire.

"Very good," commented the earl. "Go on."

"Justice," continued Tyler. "Protecting the rights of those who cannot defend themselves and upholding the law with impartiality. Sagacity. Level-headed and reasonable; having the ability to see to the heart of a matter."

"That is a most important virtue when administering justice," the earl counseled. Please continue."

"Prudence," Tyler resumed, "means to approach a situation or project with careful forethought and discretion. Knights need to exhibit good sense.

"Temperance is showing restraint or self- control."

Listening intently, the earl found himself under conviction for neglecting to develop a number of these virtues in his own life. Though he did not study to become a knight, he knew that these qualities should be exhibited by all mortals, especially those of rank.

Coming out of his revere, the earl heard Tyler say, "Resolution means to be steadfast and determined with perseverance, in other words, exhibiting tenacity."

"I have lost track of how many virtues you have elaborated on," the earl said, rather shamefacedly.

"I have listed six thus far, your lordship," Tyler replied, "Should I complete the task?"

"No need to further enumerate," answered the earl with a stifled yawn, "I can see that you have become quite proficient in your understanding and that Lord Roderick has taught you well."

Returning to the feasting, the earl dismissed all convicting thoughts of having not lived up to the ideals of his elevated position. This was a time of merriment and hobnobbing with other royals and nobility that he could impress. *"After all,"* he told himself, *"the code of chivalry is for knights, the lowest rank of nobility. Being an earl, I am above such virtues."* Filling his plate again from the bounty on the table, his lordship wandered through the gathering until he found a conversation he could join.

Garrett watched as three visiting knights, who had stood together observing the previous discussion, walked over to Tyler.

The first one began. "Let us introduce ourselves to you. I am Sir Ellison and these are my two companions, Sir Walter and Sir Kenneth. Sir Leo, our liege, brought us to your knighting event to be your tournament competitors tomorrow."

"I am pleased to meet you sirs," replied Tyler.

"Sir Kenneth and I thought to challenge you today with a fencing duel," Sir Walter continued.

"The air is quite stifling with so many stuffy dignitaries," Sir Kenneth commented."

"Yes," agreed Sir Walter. "So we thought to challenge you with a friendly duel in the courtyard."

"And what is the purpose of this duel?" asked Tyler.

"Only for some exercise and to test your knowledge when you are otherwise engaged. Anyone can recite from rote memory," answered Sir Ellison.

"This sounds like a delightful kind of sparring," Tyler responded with enthusiasm.

"I shall find us some foils," said Sir Walter.

The foursome quickly made there way out of the great hall and into the open air of the grassy courtyard.

Garrett quickly found Sekiah and told him to follow him out to the courtyard.

Overhearing Garrett talking to Sekiah, Luke, Sir Roderick's youngest page, searched for the lord to tell him of the fencing duel about to take place.

"Some spontaneous amusement to liven the day," smiled the lord.

"Shall we take our conversation outside while we watch the swordplay?" asked Sir Leo.

"A splendid idea, my friend," replied Sir Roderick.

Sir Roderick and Sir Leo came out of the great hall to find the four young combatants on the grass in the center of the courtyard by the well. A small group had already gathered to watch the interaction taking place outside.

"I am to duel *all three* of you knights at the *same* time?" Tyler asked, slightly alarmed.

"Just Sirs Walter and Kenneth," smiled Sir Ellison. I shall have my turn with you tomorrow in the tournaments!"

"Then I am still outnumbered with the two of you!" Tyler exclaimed.

"Why yes!" laughed Sir Kenneth. "We won't hurt you."

"Well, not much, anyway," sniggered Sir Walter. "Continue where you left off with the earl. I believe you were on number seven."

"En-garde!" hollered Sir Kenneth as he advanced then lunged toward Tyler with a swoosh of his foil. The two parried as each deflected the other's attack.

"You are already quite proficient with the foil," said Sir Kenneth.

"Fencing is a favourite pastime," replied the squire.

Retreating then advancing, Tyler thrust his foil toward Sir Kenneth while stating, "Truth is honesty. It is accurate and factual."

The foils clashed as Tyler deflected Sir Walter's weapon away. Tyler finished his statement. "A knight who is truthful is upright and of moral integrity."

"Very good!" Sir Leo yelled from the balcony.

Spencer and Devynne stood side by side in the gathering crowd next to Garrett and Sekiah. Sir Roderick threw out verbal encouragements to his squire.

"Liberality," the squire said next, "is showing generosity in a big-hearted way."

Both knights lunged for Tyler at the same time. He jumped back onto the low wall around the open well. Catching his breath momentarily, Tyler completed his statement. "A knight who is known for his liberality toward others is greatly loved by all."

Sir Walter and Sir Kenneth went around either side of the well thrusting their foils, but Tyler evaded the stabs by leaping off the wall and running toward the steps to the great hall.

"What is the next virtue?" hollered Sir Ellison.

"Diligence!" Tyler panted, "means to do all with careful attentiveness."

Sir Kenneth followed Tyler right up the steps. The two dueled as Sir Walter charged from below. This time Tyler could not quite escape the swishing foil without receiving a glancing blow to his arm. Although these foils were only used in practice, Tyler felt the sting of the swipe.

Tyler sparred with Sir Kenneth on the steps until he leapt onto the balcony wall and walked the distance between the pillars to the end. The other two followed but could not attack within so close a proximity to the onlookers. Just as they caught up with the squire, he swung around the post and clashed swords with Sir Walter. Dodging Sir Kenneth's lunge, Tyler dropped onto the grassy courtyard.

"Next is hope!" he yelled. "It looks forward to the future with optimism and confidence."

Bounding off the wall after Tyler, the two knights raced after him. The engagement continued with the back-and-forth play of the blades. It was all Tyler could do to continue to parry. He grew weary, but had breath enough to finish.

"Finally," the squire announced, "the twelfth and last virtue: Valour." Sir Kenneth and Sir Walter slowed their pace to allow Tyler to finish.

"The obligation of every soldier of any rank, particularly the rank of knight, is to show courage, bravery and gallantry. A knight leading his troops into battle is required to be fearless and bold. In conclusion," he said between gasps, "it is a knight's duty to wear the twelve virtues like a garment."

Both knights saluted Tyler.

"Your lord has proven to be quite thorough in his instruction with you," said Sir Walter.

"Follow his example and live by these virtues and you will become a knight of great honor," Sir Kenneth added.

The crowd of onlookers applauded and cheered for the squire.

"Good show!" shouted Spencer. "Well done!"

"You have taught your candidate well," said Sir Leo to Sir Roderick. "That was quite an impressive display on young Tyler's part."

"Your knights treated him with great sportsmanship," answered Sir Roderick."

"If he is this good tomorrow in the joust," interjected Sir Ellison, "I pity myself for competing against him!"

That brought great laughter.

𝕬pprentice-𝕶night of 𝕻rayer

𝕿he night before the dubbing ceremony, a candidate is required to spend those hours in prayer and contemplation. By exposing his soul before King Elyon, the apprentice-knight allows the Sovereign Creator to purify his heart so that when he is knighted he is found worthy for his high calling.

When evening finally came, the apprentice-knights excused themselves to the chapel. Each squire donned a white tunic to symbolize purity. Over it he wore a red cloak which stood for royalty. There they spent the entire night in prayer.

Tyler went over to the altar and knelt before the crucifix. Quietly praying, he recalled the passages of scripture of King Elyon as a warrior. He thought about the morning Sir Roderick taught the squires from the Holy Scroll on King Elyon's power.

"I saw the Lord seated on a throne,
glorious and noble,
and the train of his robe filled the temple.
Above him were seraphs, each with six wings...
They were calling to one another:
"Holy, holy, holy is the Lord,
King Elyon the Supreme;
the whole earth is full of his splendour."
At the sound of their voices the door and
thresholds shook,
and the temple became filled with smoke."

"'His train filled the temple....'Why is that significant, Tyler?" The apprentice knight recalled Sir Roderick asking.

"Because he is majestic and his train symbolizes that?" he answered.

"That sounds reasonable, except there is a better answer," came the response from the knight. "King Elyon is a warrior king and woven into the *edging of his train is the description of every battle he has ever fought – and every battle he has fought he has won!"*

Tyler pondered that thought for a long time as he thanked King Elyon for choosing him to be a knight in his realm. *"My desire is to ever be worthy of the high calling of knighthood."*

Spencer lay prostrate on the stone floor next to the outer wall. Opening his Scroll to the word of the ancient king of Israel, he read the words of David:

"King Elyon is the foundation under my feet,
the castle in which I live
my rescuing Knight. My King,
the high fortress where I run to for life.
He is my shield and my deliverer.
I sing to my King, the Praise-worthy,
and find myself safe and rescued.
Strangling cords were tight at my throat;
torrential waters rushed over me.
The ropes of death cinched me tight;
snares of death barred every exit."

"What a terrifying predicament David found himself in!" Spencer thought. He imagined himself being in that same kind of situation.

"I call to my King, I cry to King Elyon to help me.
From his palace he hears my call;
my cry brings me right into his presence!"

"King Elyon grants me a personal audience!"
Spencer mused.

"The earth trembles and heaves;
huge mountains shake,
they quake because of King Elyon's rage.
His nostrils flare, bellowing smoke;
his mouth spews forth fire.
Tongues of fire blazed out of it;
He bursts open the sky.
He steps down;
under his feet a bottomless pit opens up.
He mounts a cherubim
and soars on the wings of the wind.
He has wrapped himself in a cloak of dark clouds.
But his brightness bursts through,
spraying hailstones and fireballs.
Then King Elyon thundered out of heaven;
His voice booming!"

"Wow!" thought the squire, "What a
powerful Ruler of all heaven and earth we have!"

"The great Knight shoots his arrows,

scattering the enemy!
He hurls his lightning; they flee in retreat!"

"David's overwhelming enemy wasn't so great compared to King Elyon! They probably seemed like tiny ants compared to the Great King!"

"The depths of the ocean are exposed;
the very foundations of the earth lie uncovered
the moment You roar in protest,
letting loose Your furious rage.
Reaching all the way from sky to sea
He caught me;
He pulled me out of that drowning sea,
from my strong enemies who overpowered me."

"What a great illustration of King Elyon's jealousy for David. He loves him so much that he would go to the greatest lengths to rescue and protect him! Talk about moving heaven and earth to save one mere mortal!" Spencer pondered that revelation for a long time. "How can I comprehend that kind of love-His jealousy over me, his creation? Yet that is how I feel about Devynne. If anyone tried to harm her, I would come to her rescue in an instant! I would be her protector."

"They fought against me when I was weak,

but my King championed me on."

"*David still fought while King Elyon encouraged him,*" Spencer said to himself. "*So he would feel the satisfaction of victory. King Elyon fights alongside of us. What an amazing picture of our spiritual battles fought side-by-side our mortal combats.*"

"He brought me out into a spacious place.
I stood there saved –
rescued because King Elyon delights in me."

"*King Elyon delights in me,*" Spencer said to himself while he reflected upon the Scripture he had just read. "*That means he takes joy in me; in my calling as a knight,*" he thought to himself. "*I may need his help in battle just the way King David did.*"

Throughout the vigil, each squire consecrated himself to the service of King Elyon in knighthood. The holy presence of the King which hovered in the chapel enveloped them like a heavy blanket. Then finally the long hours of darkness gave way to the first gray light of dawn, signaling the end to a long night.

Day 2
Knighting Ceremony:
"I Dub Thee Sir Knight"

The trumpet sounded the start of a new day- *the* day. The day Tyler and Spencer had prepared their entire lives for: knighthood. The apprentice knights' first ritual this morning, bathing, signified their new purity.

Breakfast was served to the household and guests followed by morning service.

Anticipation filled the atmosphere in the great hall as the squires and pages assembled. Family and friends of the squires gathered around in small groups along with the visiting dignitaries and clergy.

The minstrels had already positioned themselves in the gallery above the screens passage (the entrance crossing the lower end of the hall between the service doors and the kitchen). The walls of the large rectangular room reached two stories high on which the heavy crossbeams of the cathedral ceiling rested. Lavish tapestries and ornate silks woven with intricate patterns lined the gray stone walls. The morning light streamed through the gigantic arched windows. Above the raised stone dais at the far end of the hall, a magnificent stained glass window glowed in brilliant colors. Its radiant reflection cast throughout the great hall. The fireplace, used primarily for warmth, was large enough to walk into. Adorned with the family coat of arms, the elaborate overmantle crafted of stone read in Latin: "....As for me and my house, we will serve King Elyon."

Lord Roderick and Lady Isabelle came from their chambers behind the dais and stood before the assembled congregation. How regal they both looked! Lady Isabelle seemed especially beautiful for this distinguished occasion in her long silk gown as she stood beaming on the dais next to Lord Roderick. The rich azure hues of her opulent garment contrasted splendidly with her flaxen hair and illuminated her twinkling bright blue eyes. Lord Roderick, a strikingly handsome man, stood fairly tall and of slender build, with dark brown hair. He sported a mustache, which Lady Isabelle said made him appear even more gallant.

The glimmer in his dark brown eyes belied the lord's serious demeanor. With shining sword at his side, Sir Roderick rested his hand around the hilt. *"How marvelous,"* he thought to himself, *"to raise these two young lads to knighthood."*

Sir Roderick's new page stood next to Devynne, Lady Isabelle's lady-in-waiting. Luke, just six years old, came to take Garrett's place now that he had become a squire.

For a brief moment, Tyler became captivated by the beautiful vision of the lovely young lady, Devynne. The brilliant scarlet and gold silk dress complimented her dark eyes and hair. She wore a simple gold head band, her hair flowing softly to her shoulders.

Then focusing his attention on the ceremony about to begin, the apprentice-knight watched as the bishop came to stand in front of Lord and Lady Bane. Bishop Donald gave a brief message honoring the apprentice knights.

"A knight spends his whole life preparing himself to be ready to fight against mortals, because there are evil mortals in the world. At the same time, he becomes trained in how to do warfare against the asmodai, which requires other complex skills. We are here to acknowledge and congratulate you squires on having mastered both!"

The two candidates stepped forward and stood in front of the dais. Sir Roderick addressed the two young soldiers before him: "By excelling in attaining each goal set before you, you have proven yourself worthy in all aspects of knighthood."

Sir Roderick then bestowed each one with gifts which held symbolic importance for the three primary facets of knighthood: religion, allegiance to the king, and the code of chivalry.

"For your proficiency in wielding the sword of Faith, I give to each of you the Sacred Scroll, which is your spiritual sword." Boldly inscribed across the front was the word, "ANOINTED", its meaning denoting the supernatural power they received from Lord Perazim to accomplish the tasks before them.

Sir Roderick continued. "I present to you a shield, representing the shield of Faith." Emblazoned on the front, a large cross indicated the great sacrifice Prince Sabaoth made for each of his subjects. In the upper left corner of the cross, the image of a chalice signified the cup of suffering that Prince Sabaoth drank. Each knight and many subjects would also receive the great honor of drinking from the chalice. In the right hand corner, a throne depicting the ruling authority that King Elyon bestowed upon Prince Sabaoth.

Sir Roderick then gifted to each a suit of armor. "When you go into mortal combat, you are reminded to also put on the whole armour of King Elyon. The spiritual armament is meant to be worn at all times, not just when going onto the battlefield."

"In remembrance of the oath that you take here today, receive your sword."

The swords were magnificent! Long, double-edged blades, glinting in the sunlight that came streaming through the windows.

"Finally," the lord said as he presented the final gift. "These spurs are given to spur you onto good works in the name of Prince Sabaoth."

Sir Roderick then led the candidates into the knight's oath. "There are two sides to uphold in the code of chivalry: justice and mercy."

The young soldiers facing Sir Roderick kneeled ready to take their oath. Together in unison they recited the code of chivalry:

"I will use my life to bring honor to our mortal sovereign, King Waymon, and to our immortal Sovereign, King Elyon and Prince Sabaoth.

I will place character above riches and concern for others above personal wealth.

I will never boast, but cherish humility.

I will speak the truth at all times and forever keep my word.

I will defend those who cannot defend themselves.

I will honor and respect women, treating older women as mothers and younger women as sisters.

I will uphold justice by showing no partiality.

I will abhor scandals and gossip by neither partaking in nor delighting in them.

I will be generous to the poor and to those who need help.

I will forgive for I have been forgiven.

I will live my life with courtesy and honor from this day forward to the honor of King Elyon and Prince Sabaoth."

Sir Roderick took his sword in both hands and solemnly raised it before him. Then lowering it, he gently touched each shoulder of the first squire as he pronounced: "I dub thee Sir Knight." He repeated the knighting ceremony for the second squire.

Sir Spencer and Sir Tyler slowly stood before Lord Roderick as the minstrels sounded the conclusion of the dubbing ceremony.

The tables were again spread with a great abundance for the banquet following the ceremony. All in attendance joyfully celebrated this happy occasion with feasting and dancing.

Garrett and Sekiah found it all so exciting that even going to bed exhausted, they both laid awake for a long time dreaming of their own knighting.

Day 3
The Tournament!

Daybreak broke upon the inhabitants of Bane Manor with the red glow of the early morning sun ushering in the promise of a day brimming with excitement. The trumpet sounded the start of the third and final day of the right of passage - the tournaments! Filled with great fanfare and pageantry the tournaments provided the opportunity for the newly dubbed knights to wear their new armor and to demonstrate their combat skills, horsemanship, and abilities with their weapons.

The bright alternating colors of the pavilions with pennants waiving cheerily on top added to the festive atmosphere. Erected around the area of the jousting field, the round tents housed the combatants and physicians.

Lord and Lady Bane sat in the center of the berfrois, the stands overlooking the jousting arena, called the lists. Soon the berfrois filled with other ladies and nobles including the participant's families.

The lists, being in close proximity to the castle, allowed the servants the opportunity to view the events from atop the battlements. The field surrounding the tournament overflowed with spectators from the surrounding villages and towns.

While the commoners stood around the perimeter of the list waiting for the start of the day's events, jugglers, minstrels and dancers moved about entertaining the crowd. Geoffrey, the burly blacksmith, loved to amuse with his limericks. His deep strong voice arrested the attention of a group of peasants.

"There once was a girl from Bane,
Who sadly looked quite plain;
Her father did sigh,
He tried not to cry,
But her looks just could not be changed."

The crowd booed and hissed in merriment. "That's terrible!" Someone heckled in fun.

"Ah, me fine fellow," Geoffrey replied good naturedly, "there be more. Listen. This rhyme is for the womenfolk."

"In time the girl from Bane,
Grew up no longer looking the same;
Her father did cry,
'What a beauty have I,'
All the lads will want my dame!"

The women clapped and laughed with approval.

"Go on ye," said a grandmother loudly standing close by, "you redeem yerself with that verse!"

> "Now this same woman from Bane,
> Who had an intelligent brain;
> She did not agree,
> Remained resolute like a tree,
> But her protest was proved in vain.

> "One day the lady from Bane,
> Went out to walk on the plain;
> When along came a knight,
> Who fought a great fight,
> That he should give her his name."

With a blast, the bugler trumpeted the signal that the pageantry had begun. Cheers from the enthusiastic throng rose up to greet the judges and contestants entering the arena in formal procession riding their steeds in full regalia.

A hush fell over the crowd as Bishop Donald stepped forward to offer the invocation.

"Great King Elyon," intoned the bishop. "We beseech thee to look favourably upon this festive day and to protect all here from accident or harm. May all those in attendance keep the spirit of this day during these tournaments. For this we thank thee."

Stepping back, the bishop returned to his place in the stands. The crier moved to the forefront to announce the event and to remind the knights of their chivalric code of conduct.

"Hear ye now, me lords and ladies; good citizens all!" bellowed the herald. "On this momentous occasion I announce the contestants and rules for this tournament. In this the final stage of receiving knighthood are Sir Spencer and Sir Tyler. To challenge these knights, are Sir Ellison, Sir Kenneth and Sir Walter.

"The rules are simple: To score points, a clean hit to the center of the shield is required or by unseating your opponent. If the combatant strikes either rider or horse, you are disqualified."

Trumpets blared as the riders retreated to their respective stations. The first contest pitted Sir Spencer against Sir Ellison.

Sir Spencer carried the glove of his sweetheart, Devynne. He spied her in the gallery; the gossamer fabric floating from her cone-shaped hat fluttered in the soft breeze; her dark beauty urged him even more so to prove his skill.

Sekiah stood at the ready next to Sir Spencer to assist him with his gear and to hand him his lance.

Drums rolled in steady rhythm; excitement mounted! The herald signaled the charge.

Digging their spurs into the sides of their mounts the competitors rushed forth. Dust flew from under the pounding hooves that reverberated against the earth like thunder. Nostrils flared as each horse raced toward the other. Both opposing knight leveled his lance focusing on the other's shield. Crrrack! The tremendous jolt of hitting the mark shattered the lance. Shards flew in all directions. For a breathless moment, the helpless knight appeared suspended in space before crashing into the soft dirt, losing his helmet as his lance hurtled through the air. Sir Spencer unseated his opponent! The crowd erupted into wild cheers. Devynne beamed with joy at the victory of her gallant knight while wildly waving her lace handkerchief.

Sir Ellison's squire ran onto the field to help him up, gather the remnants of his splintered lance, and retrieve the knight's helmet.

During the lull in action, while the combatants changed, the entertainers once again performed for the crowd. Geoffrey delighted the gathering around him with another limerick.

"There once was a knight on his way,
To find a joust he could play;

To fight with his might,
was such a delight,
He lived to join in the fray.

"The knight on his way,
Had a horse who would stray,
For he only wanted some hay;
The knight on his horse,
Corrected his course,
And finally found his way."

Everyone laughed at Geoffrey's clever lines.

Suddenly the staccato notes of the bugler signaled that the tournament was about to begin again. The herald cried out to the spectators that the joust would take place between Sir Tyler and Sir Kenneth. Garrett handed Sir Tyler his lance.

Facing each other, the knights waited for the signal. Again, the drums built the spectator's anticipation. The herald signaled the charge. Dashing toward each other, the warriors leveled their lances.

"It's a clean miss-!" announced the crier. "Neither weapon hit!"

Turning around, the horses snorted as the two charged again with great fury. Sir Kenneth struck Sir Tyler on the shoulder; but Sir Tyler hit his target dealing a great blow, disintegrating his lance into pieces. Sir Kenneth flew off his horse, landing with forceful clanging.

Sir Spencer and Sir Tyler completed the afternoon's tournament, each winning two rounds and each losing one round. It was a most exhilarating day!

All the warriors went back to their pavilions to have their bruises and sore muscles attended to.

The evening stars appeared as the last light of the setting sun faded into the night sky. In the great hall the air was filled with appetizing smells from the elaborate banquet and the sound of laughter and lively conversation. All in attendance wore their finest attire.

Soon the sweet strains of a violin could be heard accompanying the clear notes of a flute calling the nobles and their ladies to the floor. The rest of the minstrels joined in the music and the first dance of the evening began. Both Garrett and Sekiah found partners. Sir Spencer sought out Devynne. Escorting her to the floor, he told her how beautiful she looked.

"You look quite stunning this evening, my lady," Sir Spencer remarked admiringly. "The deep blue in your gown almost looks like purple."

"Thank you," Devynne replied shyly.

"Periwinkle is my favourite colour."

"I hope to have every dance with you tonight," she said.

"Your wish is my command, my lady!" Sir Spencer said with a dramatic bow and flourish of his hand.

"Do you suppose we could also take a short walk in the night air to look at the stars?" Devynne said gazing up into his deep blue eyes.

"We can certainly do that before the evening is over," Sir Spencer said, taking her small hand in his strong one as he guided her into a circle of couples already moving together in rhythm.

Sir Tyler watched from the side as he made conversation with the knights from the tournament.

"Ah, there you are our friend and worthy compatriot!" Sir Tyler heard through the din of the music and voices all around. Turning to his left, he spied his three opponents from the duel and jousting tournament.

"How can you be enjoying this last evening of festivities merely by observing?" asked Sir Walter. "You are a man of action!"

"Yes," interjected Sir Kenneth, "you must needs find a partner and dance!

"My prowess is on the battlefield, my good knights," replied Sir Tyler. "The dance floor is not for me."

The Hunt

Chapter 6

The predawn light stealthily crept over the eastern sky pushing the night away. An early morning chill and the dampness from the night's steady rain hung in the air. Winter had passed, but spring came ever so slowly. The thrill of receiving knighthood now belonged in the annals of history.

Sir Roderick had called a hunt for the day. He departed the manor with his hunting party sometime after the huntsman and his rache handlers. The huntsman and his handlers went ahead using the hounds to sniff out the game. Sir Roderick's party included Sirs Spencer and Tyler along with Garrett and Sekiah. Luke rode excitedly along on his first hunt.

Riding next to Luke, Sir Roderick went over the terminology of hunting with his young page. "An important accomplishment of your training for eventual knighthood is to know and understand all aspects of the hunt," Sir Roderick instructed. "Have you been memorizing the terms that I gave you?" he asked.

"Yes, Sir Roderick," Luke replied confidently. "I studied them again last night just in case you asked me today."

"I am pleased to know that you are prudently studying your lessons, Luke," said the knight. "This is a good time for you to tell me what you know."

"There are eight parts to a hunt," the page began. "The quest: The huntsman seeks out the quarry with his special hunting dog, called a lymer, before the hunt begins. Two, assembly is when the hunting party meets to go over the huntsman's findings and decide how to undertake the hunt. This is decided over breakfast. Third, the relay is where the raches are stationed along the path the hart is expected to flee. This way the dogs won't be worn out. Fourth is moving, where the lymer is used to track down the hart. Fifth is the chase, which is the actual hunt. Sixth is when the hart can no longer run and turns to try and defend itself. It's called....I know what it is....think...think...think...." The lad said to himself, thumping his forehead with his fist trying to jog his memory.

"You are doing quite well, Luke," commended Sir Roderick. Do you need some help?"

"Baying!" Luke said with relief and satisfaction that he could recall the term. "This is when you or one of the other knights makes the kill. Seven is unmaking," the page continued. "That is when the deer is field dressed by the woodsman. Cure'e is number eight. The dogs get to have some pieces of the carcass. It must be done in a way so they know it is a reward for their work."

"What part of the hunt are we on?" Garrett asked Luke.

"We are on number Two," Luke stated. "I'm hungry and can't wait to eat!"

The others in the party laughed. "

"There's the huntsman now!" cried Garrett. "I'm hungry, too."

Breakfast over and the decision made for the location of the hunt, the party saddled up and headed to the far side of Lord Roderick's forest. The huntsman and the rache handlers had already gone ahead and stationed the hounds in pairs to run a relay along the expected path of the deer.

Awhile later, the group came upon the area of their hunt. The forest showed the first signs of new life in the undergrowth and on the trees. The meadow spread before them rose and fell like gentle swells on a calm sea. A stream cut through a swath of the prairie grass and sapling as it meandered on its way to a distant lake. A herd of deer grazed peacefully in the field.

The huntsman blew his horn and the raches ran barking with all their might. The herd bolted in all directions going deep into the forest. A hart and a stag ran straight toward the path of the hounds. The dogs gave chase in relay form until the red deer became too weary to continue their flight. The horses and riders bounded through the meadow and sailed across the stream into the forest. Galloping along with the hounds, they jumped over fallen logs and ducked low limbs. Slowing down, the hunters reached for their quiver, drew their bow, took aim, and let fly the arrows! The stag fell, but the hart with an arrow lodged in its neck and another in its flank dashed away back toward the stream again and into a thicket of saplings. The grand chase resumed as horses' hooves thundered through the woods. Sir Roderick and Sir Spencer joined the hounds in hot pursuit. Reaching the other side of the stream, the hounds tracked the buck by its trail of blood and surrounded the game just as it went down. Sir Roderick and Sir Spencer arrived with the barking dogs to the fallen hart, both feeling exhilarated from the chase. In the meantime, Sir Tyler trotted across the meadow to the stag.

Luke stayed behind with the woodsman during the hunt, but now the woodsman took over to field dress the deer. Luke and the huntsman rode over to where the dogs received their cure'e. Off in the distance, the huntsman noticed some colorful fabric near the road. Curiosity overcame the hunter, so he trotted over to investigate. Luke, not one to miss out on a new discovery, caught up with the huntsman. To their dismay, they found a body lying face down in some decaying leaves. Shocked at the sight, the two dismounted and Luke helped the huntsman turn the body over. Surprised to hear a low groan coming from the wounded mortal, the startled huntsman blew his horn to summon Sir Roderick. The lord trotted over and dismounted to take a look at the wounded mortal.

"He is wet and muddy from the night's rain," the knight observed, taking off his surcoat to put around the unconscious mortal.

While Sekiah watched the hounds enjoying their reward, he felt overcome by the strong presence of Lord Perazim. Suddenly a vision overtook his awareness. He saw Vikings ambush two unsuspecting riders sent from Brighton Castle, messengers of King Waymon, sovereign of all Britanniae. This one left for dead; the other taken away to a far distant land. They could not go after him. Sekiah felt no fear, only the importance of telling Sir Roderick the vision.

The sky had cleared from the morning clouds. Devynne took her needlework outside to enjoy while sitting on the battlement. Suddenly a strong urging in her spirit compelled her to make things ready for someone seriously wounded. Bewildered, Devynne contemplated the feeling. Finally, she took her work in and searched for Lady Isabelle.

"I can't tell you why, m'lady," Devynne began, "but I have a strong urge to ready things for someone terribly wounded; perhaps in the hunt."

"Devynne," replied Lady Isabelle, "we know that unexplained unctions are usually from Lord Perazim, and we must hearken to his instructions. I have a similar sense, myself."

"Please, King Elyon," Devynne pleaded, "do not let it be Sir Spencer!" Then looking over at Lady Isabelle, she added, "Nor Lord Roderick, either!"

Lady Isabelle smiled. "I don't know what to expect, Devynne, but I do not think we are preparing for the expected."

Sir Roderick blew his bugle, calling for the woodsman. The huntsman took over his work so the woodsman could ride over to the site of much distress.

"We need for you to make a litter to transport this poor mortal back to the Manor," Sir Roderick instructed.

The squires helped the woodsman make a make-shift litter and carefully strapped the mortal onto it.

"Garrett," Sir Roderick ordered, "I need for you and Sekiah to go on ahead to get Dr. Galen and bring him to the Manor."

The journey home went very slowly, but the way proved rough for someone injured.

"I see that you are in very serious contemplation, lad." Sir Roderick commented to Luke. "Are you troubled?"

"Yes, m'lord," Luke replied. "Did King Elyon create evil?"

"That is a mighty deep question for one so young. What prompts you to ask?" inquired the lord.

"This mortal and his companion were sent on an errand, and they were waylaid by Vikings – at least that is what Sekiah said. Why would King Elyon allow that if he is only good?" asked the page.

"King Elyon is only good, Luke," stressed the knight. "He did not create evil. He created all celestial beings and mortals with the choice to love and serve him or not. Asmo chose not to. Now he tries to cause mortals not to as well. Evil is not the opposite of good. Evil is the absence of good. There is a very big difference, my boy," concluded Sir Roderick.

"But why would King Elyon let such a terrible thing like this happen?" Luke persisted.

"This I can tell you, King Elyon's ways are not like ours," answered Sir Roderick. "There are times when something that seems terrible might not be after all when we learn the whole story. Do you remember the story of Sir Ivan from the third Crusade?" he asked.

"I have not heard that story yet," replied the young page.

"Many years ago," began the lord, "a troop of knights journeyed to the Holy Land. During their travels they encountered a skirmish, and Sir Ivan and his fellow soldiers were captured by the enemy. During his imprisonment," the lord continued, "the knight began having dreams from Lord Perazim concerning calamities that would soon overtake the realm. At first, the other prisoners laughed at him. However, when Sir Ivan's dreams began to come to pass, the jailor took note of the knight's warnings concerning the calamities. He informed the ruling prince of Sir Ivan's dreams in order to warn the monarch of impending disasters in his principality. The prince heeded all that Sir Ivan spoke."

The young page listened intently to Sir Roderick's story.

"The prince made a decree to all the subjects that they were to do exactly as the knight commanded," Sir Roderick said. "And Sir Ivan saved the lives of the entire nation!"

"When the crisis ended," Sir Roderick concluded. "The prince granted the knight any wish he desired."

"What did he ask for?" Luke asked.

"He asked for his fellow soldiers to be released from prison and allowed to return home."

"Did Sir Ivan return home, too?" asked the page.

"No," answered Sir Roderick. "He had been made second in command of the entire realm and given the prince's daughter to marry."

"Do you think the mortal will save his enemies like Sir Ivan?" asked Luke.

"We do not know yet why this happened, but Lord Perazim spoke to Sekiah to tell us that he knows the whole story. In the meantime, we are not to be afraid of the Vikings, and we are to ask King Elyon to take care of the unfortunate companion who was kidnapped."

Long after nightfall the hunting party arrived back at the Manor. Lady Isabelle, with the help of Devynne, had everything ready and waiting to minister to the young mortal lying before them.

"Bring him over here, next to the fire," the doctor ordered Sirs Spencer and Tyler, who carried him into the great hall on the litter.

Janie brought hot water over from the fireplace for Lady Isabelle. Devynne assisted both women in washing the wounds of the unconscious mortal.

Many deep bruises discoloured the skin. Sir Roderick helped Dr. Galen set his broken arm. A low groan came forth and scowl crossed the injured mortal's face. The gash on the back of his head where the Viking clubbed him and knocked him out proved difficult to clean. As the women gingerly worked to wash the blood and filth away from his matted, dirty hair, low moans escaped his breath.

"I have done all I can for this young mortal," Dr. Galen said, standing up and stretching. He needs to be watched overnight.

"I shall take the first watch," Janie offered.

"Luke will escort you to your room, Dr. Galen," Sir Roderick said.

"Thank you," the doctor replied as he followed the young page.

The rest of the household, weary from a long day, retired to their beds for the night.

The Prank

Chapter 7

When morning arrived, Sir Roderick took over the vigil. He called for his knight-errants, Sir Spencer and Sir Tyler.

"Since we surmise that this poor soul travelled forth from Brighton Castle with a message from King Waymon, I send you back to tell his lordship concerning the incident. I need for you and your squires to ready yourselves for the journey the morrow after next. I would like to wait a day in case the poor lad awakens and we may discover the nature of his errand and his name and that of his companion. In the meantime, I will go over the route with you."

"Yes, your lordship," both knights said in unison.

"Our first errand!" Sir Tyler said to his companion as they departed for the stables.

Bishop Donald passed them by on his way to sit with Sir Roderick for a bit. "Good morning, Sir Roderick," he greeted the lord upon approaching the knight. "I have been in conversation with King Elyon for this young mortal and his companion that they would both live and not die. I am at peace that in spite of this dreadful incident, his Sovereign even manages to work all things together for the good of those who serve him. In time we may even be privileged to learn of his purpose."

"Yes, bishop," Sir Roderick responded. "It does seem unrighteous of King Elyon to allow these things to come upon his servants, but then we live in a fallen world...."

"King Elyon has promised his protection," Bishop Donald picked up where Sir Roderick left off. "But even so, we see examples in the Holy Scroll where his most faithful friends and servants did not always receive that protection. King Elyon sometimes had a higher purpose for allowing the suffering and even the death of his saints."

"'Tis a weighty matter to contemplate, indeed," Sir Roderick concluded. "To lighten the heavy mood," he said, changing the subject. "I have been devising a scheme to play upon my young errant-knights and their squires. We are approaching April 1st and the time for mischief-making."

"I know you, my lord," said the bishop. "Your reputation for pranks is unparalleled! Count me in if you need assistance in the hoax."

"I'm glad that you offered, bishop," Sir Roderick said with glee, "because you are exactly the one I need to carry out my prank!"

"A little levity is like a good medicine to the soul," the bishop said with a smile. It took the rest of the day for Bishop Donald to have everything ready.

In the late afternoon, just before the evening meal, Dr. Galen came around to check on his patient. He could see that his instructions had been carried out with great care.

"Ah, Dr. Galen," Lady Isabelle greeted, as she came into the grand hall. "Please join us for supper."

"Thank you, Lady Isabelle, I would be most happy to," the doctor replied.

Devynne took her turn watching the patient while the rest of the household ate. Sitting by the fire she worked diligently on her needlework. Setting it down on her lap for a brief moment, Devynne noticed the mortal stirring. He seemed to be restless as if trying to awaken.

"Dr. Galen!" she called quietly, "the patient rouses."

Soon the herald spoke. He confirmed Sekiah's vision and gave his name as Cedric; his companion's name was Cole. The doctor gave Cedric a tonic to help him rest through the night. They would learn more in the morning.

The trumpet sounded the call of a new day. The dim morning light shrouded in a deep hazy mist caused the castle to appear ghost-like.

"Perfect." Bishop Donald said to himself, "Now to pull this off!"

After morning chapel, the household dispersed to start their day. Sir Roderick lingered, as if in earnest consultation with King Elyon. Luke stood by waiting to receive his orders from the lord. Bishop Donald told the four soldiers that he wished to speak to them before they departed on their first journey, so they came to the front of the chapel.

"Luke," the bishop addressed the young page. "Sir Roderick is preoccupied at the moment, so you may wait for him in the kitchen. Find out if Janie needs your assistance.

Turning to the lads, the bishop started to say something. But before he could begin, a strange sound escaped Sir Roderick. Everyone stopped and looked inquisitively at him.

"I wrestle not against flesh and blood!" the knight said struggling to speak.

Eight pairs of eyes widened in shock at the spectacle. Lord Roderick fell to the floor writhing as if in a wrestling match. "I bind you, Asmo!" he said with force.

"Quick!" said Sir Spencer to Bishop Donald, "we need your Scroll!"

Bishop Donald went to the podium to retrieve it, but it wasn't there. Going to his office, he heard the young knights speaking loudly with authority in the secret language over Sir Roderick.

"Unrhyw arf a ffurfiwyd yn erbyn Rhaid i chi yn ffynnu!" cried Sir Spencer with determination.

"Aucune arme forgée contre toi sera sans effet!" Sir Tyler stated firmly.

"We know what to do," Sekiah said to Garrett. He sang a battle song while Garrett danced along. Stomping and clapping, Garrett jumped and gyrated in rhythm to Sekiah's song.

Returning from his office, Sir Tyler took the Scroll and began to read aloud portions pertaining to spiritual warfare.

Just then, Sir Roderick jumped up and ran to the back of the sanctuary, hollering, "I see ghosts in the mist!"

Sir Tyler ran to the doors to close them so the lord would not run out. Bishop Donald fled into his office so as not to laugh out loud. Garrett and Sekiah looked at each other bewildered. The bishop came back out with a vial of holy oil. Tipping a drop onto his index finger, Bishop Donald went over to Sir Roderick.

"NO!" shrieked the knight, "Not that!"

"Come out, you disgusting asmodai!" the bishop ordered. Taking his finger with the oil on it, he touched the lord's forehead.

With that, Sir Roderick slumped onto Sir Tyler and Bishop Donald who led him to a bench close by.

Lord Roderick winked at Bishop Donald. "We pulled it off!" exclaimed the knight. "What jolly amusement!"

Both knight and bishop burst into a fit of hearty laughter.

"My lord," said the bishop between guffaws, "You are quite the actor!"

"My young warriors," Sir Roderick said, "You have now been initiated into the Bane Manor jokes of fame!"

"None of this was real?" asked Garrett in surprise.

"No," answered the bishop.

"But if ever I trained some stout warriors, you fellas are certainly that!" said the knight. "It has been a long time since I pulled a prank. With all the heaviness since yesterday, this seemed to be the time for some harmless fun."

"You certainly outwitted us, Sir Roderick!" smiled Sir Tyler.

"Now we have to learn when it's real and when it's false," said Sekiah.

"It can be difficult to discern, at first," said Bishop Donald. "But with experience and time spent with King Elyon, He will send Lord

Perazim to quickly tell you what is really taking place."

Throughout the day, Cedric revealed a little more each time he awoke.

"Cole and I are heralds for King Waymon," he began. "We were sent out this time to announce a tournament at Brighton Castle."

"When is the tournament to be held?" inquired Sir Roderick.

"On the ides of April, your lordship," Cedric answered.

"A little more than a fortnight," Sir Roderick said to himself. "By that time you should be well enough to travel with us."

Seeing the look of sorrow pass across the mortal's countenance, Sir Roderick comforted the lad. "Do not grieve for your friend, for King Elyon has sent him to a distant land on another mission for his kingdom's sake."

"Then why did he leave me behind?" asked the herald.

"King Elyon's wisdom is full of mysteries; some for us to know and some for us to merely trust," came the wise reply.

Sir Roderick wrote a message for his knights to deliver to King Waymon and went over the route with Sir Spencer and Sir Tyler. He made certain that his knight-errants and their squires had all the necessities for their journey.

"You should be gone no longer than a week, at the very most," Sir Roderick stated. "We will beseech King Elyon to give you safe travel until you return. Greet those who give you lodging on my behalf."

Sir Spencer easily located his sweetheart, Devynne, in the music room practicing the flute. The young suitor paused just outside the doorway to listen to the beautiful piece she played. Upon hearing the last note, the young knight entered the room.

"Good afternoon, sweet Devynne!" he greeted with a slight flourish.

A rosy blush tinged her cheeks as her heart gave a little thrill of delight at her young suitor's presence. Devynne smiled as she put her instrument down.

"What pleasure is mine to have your company," she said, putting her music away.

"Lord Roderick is sending Sir Tyler and me with our squires on an errand to Brighton Castle."

"I expected as much since the king needs to know what has become of his heralds," Devynne replied.

"My comrades and I leave at first light," Sir Spencer stated.

"This will be your first errand away from Bane Manor," Devynne said wistfully.

"I am full of adventure as any young knight would be, m'lady," Sir Spencer replied. "The parting between us I do not relish, and despite the anticipation of the journey, I already long to see your lovely face when I return."

"I shall mope about the castle while you are away," answered Devynne.

"Oh my lady," Sir Spencer exclaimed. "You must encourage me with your fortitude and by continually calling upon King Elyon to protect and help me! One reason I admire you is for your devotion to our great Sovereign."

"What other reasons do you admire me for?" the young lady-in-waiting inquired.

"You are also devoted to your cousin, Lady Isabelle," answered Sir Spencer. "You are kind to the pages and other children at the manor."

"Are your reasons complete?" she asked.

"No, m'lady," the young knight replied. "I have not even begun. Alas and alack, I have neither the wit nor the time to beguile you with words of my esteem."

"'Tis better for you to refrain or I might become vain and conceited by your flattery," Devynne stated feeling a bit uncomfortable. "I did ask but that can lead us into forbidden territory."

Quickly changing the subject, Devynne asked, "How long do you imagine to be away on this errand?"

"Sir Roderick thought perhaps a week," Sir Spencer answered.

"Such a long week it shall be for me, too!" exclaimed Devynne. "But I will stay occupied and will continually talk to King Elyon on your behalf."

"That, sweet Devynne," Sir Spencer finished, "will give me strength on my errand."

The two departed the music room to join the rest of the household in time for supper.

Captured by the Asmodai

Chapter 8

𝔙aliant plodded easily along the dirt path. Garrett enjoyed the muffled sound of his horse's hooves as they rhythmically kicked up the dust, keeping with the pace of the peaceful afternoon. The meandering stream gently rippled under the branches of the broad shade trees. The spring leaves softened the brightness of the dappled sunbeams so that rider and horse enjoyed the cool, tranquil day.

Since they now accompanied the knight-errants on journeys and into battle, Sir Roderick, without fanfare, provided Garrett and Sekiah their own sword and shield and horse; the typical Rouncey used for travel and battle.

In addition to his battle gear, Sekiah also received his own set of banners he would need in case they came under attack by the asmodai or forced into mortal combat.

On this errand, the knights and squires wore chain mail under their embroidered tunics, which bore emblems signifying their liege lord.

The knight's tunics, more intricately woven, showed their rank. Since Vikings had come to Britanniae, Sir Roderick took extra precautions sending his message to King Waymon with soldiers, not by herald.

Sekiah sang joyfully as he rode in front of Garrett. The squire rejoiced in the fine horse he named "Song of Judah," but simply called "Judah." He chose that name because "Judah" means praise. Sekiah's heart loved to sing praises to King Elyon.

"So," remarked Sir Spencer. "Our liege has sent along with us a crooning squire to keep us company and to warn all mortals and beasts who might be near!"

"This may prove to be a good thing or it may make for a very long journey!" Sir Tyler said jokingly.

That night the four made camp and slept under the stars, grateful for the tranquil weather.

The asmodai watched and observed. Taking notes and assessing the attitudes and strengths of the youths, they plotted schemes to trap them. These young toughs, untried in real life, would fall easily into their hands. Scurrying away, the invisible enemy salivated over their plans.

The soldiers made good time the second day. By mid afternoon the fortress came into view from across the expansive plain. Sir Leo the Dragon-Slayer and the knights from Sirs Spencer and Tyler's celebration lived there.

Being still a distance a way, the band came upon a caravan of wandering Keltoi. As the nomads busied themselves around a fire getting ready to settle in for the night, the chieftain stepped forward.

"I see that you mighty soldiers have traveled a fare piece and must be hungry and weary by now," he said in his most gracious manner. "It would be our great honour to invite you to share in our humble supper!"

"We are on our way to the fortress yonder," replied Sir Spencer.

"You have plenty of time to reach the fortress before nightfall," the chieftain answered.

"'Tis true that we feel a bit hungry and weary from the long day in the saddle, so we accept," Sir Spencer acknowledged.

It felt good to dismount and stretch a bit. The chieftain ushered the two knights over to the fire while the squires tied up the horses to some nearby trees.

Sekiah, ever vigilant, remained on guard. He knew from his training that it was imperative to never let his defenses down. As they approached the group, Sekiah whispered to Garrett to stay on the alert as well. The squires glanced around at the various activities going on. The women worked alongside some of the girls as they guided them in preparing the food. One of the menfolk had taken a few boys into the forest to fetch more firewood. A minstrel slowly strolled weaving his way in and around the various small groups and by the fire while softly strumming his lute. A grandmother sat rocking a crying infant as she told stories to some young children gathered around her. Sekiah saw the look of interest on their faces and wandered over to listen to what the old woman said.

"When I was your age," the old woman said, speaking with an air of great confidentiality. "My grandmother taught me the secrets of the crystal ball, which knows all. Now I will tell you." Eagerly the children drew closer. The infant began to quiet down as it nestled into her shoulder. The grandmother picked up the glass orb and held it in her lap.

Sekiah looked at Garrett and found him standing intensely fascinated, observing a sorcerer casting an hypnotic spell on a girl as several other children looked on in amazement. The magician caused the child to perform acts impossible for mortals to do. Fire flew off her fingertips, and she could stand suspended several feet in the air with nothing supporting her!

"Fluri is levitating!" the magician stated with satisfaction. Some commands brought laughter to the other children. The magician brought her down to the ground and woke her up.

"Fluri, do you know what just happened to you?" one of the children asked.

"No," the girl answered rather weakly. "I feel like I'm just waking up."

"Who should I choose next?" the sorcerer asked scanning the faces of his eager young audience. "This time it is not to demonstrate only, but to train you how to levitate."

Breaking his concentration, Garrett noticed that Sekiah had come over to him. Both knew instinctively that they should leave this camp right away. Sorcery and witchcraft were flashy imitations of the real power that came from Prince Sabaoth.

"What should we do?" whispered Garrett.

Their eyes quickly scanned around the fire, looking for Sir Spencer and Sir Tyler. The knights, clearly engaged in conversation with their host, seemed unaware of the kind of caravan they had come across. Somehow, the squires had to interrupt so they could leave.

Just as Garrett began to walk over to where the knights stood, he felt the heavy, dark presence of the asmodai lurking nearby. Sekiah also perceived the cold rush of their movement. Approaching Sir Spencer, Garrett noticed a strange, glassy-eyed look. He could see that the young soldier had let his guard down! Even a knight who had received a lifetime of training could neglect to put on his spiritual armour.

Sir Tyler had a quizzical expression on his face. He did not quite know what to think of the occurrences going on around him. The conversation with the chieftain distracted him from paying close attention to the unusual activities. However, Sir Tyler felt increasingly uncomfortable associating with this group of Keltois. He indicated to Sir Spencer that they should not stay for supper but continue onto the fortress.

Sir Spencer, annoyed at this suggestion, declared, "We have already accepted their generous offer of hospitality, and we cannot now offend our hosts. There will be plenty of time to make it to the fortress before nightfall," he stated defiantly to the rest of his group.

"Perhaps the others should go on ahead," proposed the chieftain, in his most charming manner. "It is not far from here, and there is still plenty of daylight left by which to reach the fortress," he insisted. "It is not often that we humble Keltoi have the privilege of serving the nobility right in our own camp."

"*Nobility.*" That term pleased Sir Spencer in his new rank as a knight.

"Besides, Sir Knight," the chieftain went on, using his most flattering references to Sir Spencer's position. "Our conversation had not yet ended. You were telling me the most interesting story."

Sir Spencer, without realizing the manipulative tactics used by the chieftain, accepted the invitation extended to him.

"The rest of you go on, and I will catch up before dark," Sir Spencer ordered. "Garrett, there is no need for you to attend me until I come to the fortress later."

Garrett and Sekiah looked at each other with alarm in their eyes. Sir Tyler understood the futility of trying to persuade Sir Spencer any further. The three untied their horses and mounted up. Galloping at full speed toward the fortress, the knight and squires knew they needed reinforcements to rescue their comrade.

Returning to his host, Sir Spencer reiterated the chieftains' remarks, "There is plenty of time to reach the fortress before nightfall."

"Did I say that you would reach the fortress before nightfall?" the chieftain asked.

Sir Spencer nodded as he looked quizzically at his host. "That may be what you thought you heard me say, but that is not what I said. I said you *might* reach the fortress before nightfall. Perhaps you should stay the night with us."

"That was confusing," Sir Spencer thought to himself. *"Of course I heard the chieftain correctly the first time. Didn't I? Perhaps not."*

The late afternoon sun cast deep shadows in the woods. The flickering firelight caused everyone around the camp to look unnatural. The conversations going on around seemed to make little sense. Sitting on the ground against a log in front of the bonfire, Sir Spencer attempted to act normal as he conversed with several inquisitive children. He began to feel slightly dizzy. The unusual aromas of incense burning and mystic incantations in the background caused his mind to whirl in confusion.

A young maiden filled his plate full of meats with unusual spices. He couldn't quite decide if he liked the flavours or not. Sir Spencer reeled in utter disorientation. By the end of supper he found himself unable to think clearly about anything!

The strange music playing incessantly in the background; the incantations the women chanted...the perplexing odors wafting through the air...the bizarre behaviours and conversations going on around seemed to cloud his mind...

The asmodai made their move. Sir Spencer found himself surrounded with no strength of will to resist.

Into the Caverns of Cataclysmic Calamities

Chapter 9

There were only gray shadows. No color. The air grew increasingly dank and foul as the asmodai compelled the knight deeper and deeper into the caverns. The pale glow emanating from the slime oozing down the walls gave off the faintest light revealing beetles scuttling to and fro. Bats clung to the hanging stalactites and tiny spiders crawled across the pathway. Sir Spencer shivered in the cold and clammy cave. He felt completely disoriented and miserable. Although the knight heard many unearthly voices, he could not see anyone. The unnerving darkness and awareness of his utter aloneness crushed his spirit. Despair overwhelmed the knight.

The hideous voices that echoed all around taunting him caused Sir Spencer to grimace in distress. *"What kind of knight lets himself get captured by the asmodai?"* they said.

"My comrades have abandoned me.... I not

only let myself down, but also my companions and Lord Roderick. Devynne, my sweet Devynne will not love me when she learns of my folly." Sir Spencer continued agreeing with the words that floated around him. Thoughts of blame and self-pity intermingled, accompanied by screams of agony and gleeful shrills of laughter which intensified his ordeal. On and on this went.

"Is this death?" Sir Spencer wondered. *"No, this is not death. Perhaps it would be better to be dead."* The perplexed knight reasoned. If this is not the Gehenna of Judgment, *then Gehenna must surely be more frightening than anything I am able to imagine!"*

Looking down, Sir Spencer tried to step around the frigid pools of slime, but the knight could not keep from slipping into some of the slick puddles. Vigorously shaking off his soaking wet shoe, he felt the sudden sting of icy cold water drip from a stalactite down the back of his neck momentarily taking his breath away, chilling him to the bone.

While Sir Spencer suffered the torments of the cavern, his companions sped across the plain on their horses toward the fortress. Sekiah waved the red flag, alerting the sentry they needed help from the soldiers. The same flag also indicated their allegiance to King Elyon's realm.

The gate opened and Sir Tyler quickly explained to the sentry the plight of their comrade. The sentry trumpeted the alarm calling the knights to arms and raised the orange flag signaling warfare. Sir Leo the Dragonslayer, in charge of the fortress, came to meet the soldiers.

"Sir Spencer fell into the trap of the Keltoi," explained Sir Tyler.

"I know their ploys," answered Sir Leo. "They work their wiles to lead mortals to the Caverns of Cataclysmic Calamities."

"Why?" Garrett asked dismayed.

"The Keltois believe they need a sacrifice for the dragons to insure its favour," said Sir Leo.

"Favour for what?" asked Sekiah.

"Their magick," replied the knight. "They think the dragons bring them good luck. It is a trick that the asmodai play on the Keltoi. We must sally forth to save the young knight from certain peril!"

Sir Leo dispatched a sentry to Beste Abbey nearby to let them know that they headed into combat on a rescue mission so the sisters would be ready to care for any injured soldiers.

Before leaving the fortress, Sir Leo admonished the soldiers to put their spiritual armor on as well.

"Listen, men," Sir Leo bellowed. "This is not a battle against only mortals. We are going to bring back a knight who has been captured by the asmodai. You must be extremely careful to keep your shield raised at all times because the Keltois, who are in league with Asmo, will do everything they can to cause you to lower it. If you do, you will become an immediate casualty yourself!" the skilled knight admonished the soldiers as he rode down the line so all could hear.

"This is the most important kind of battle we ever fight - rescuing a subject of King Elyon! We do this in the name of Prince Sabaoth!!" roared Sir Leo.

Shields raised, the army marched out onto the field before them. In conflicts like this, Sir Bruce the Worship Warrior led the way. Brandishing the flag ahead of them, he called out the victory chant of Prince Sabaoth. The entire force shouted in deafening unison. Sekiah followed directly behind Sir Bruce.

"We are marching for our King –
King Elyon!
No weapon formed against us –
can harm us!
Lord Perazim goes on ahead –
to help us!
We will overcome them –
by Prince Sabaoth!"

The look-out for the Keltois had watched the changing of the flag on the fortress and warned the others of the approaching army. Staying hidden among the trees, the women worked their magic spells and incantations while the men positioned themselves in another area to ambush the approaching regiment by shooting their flaming arrows.

As long as the knights and squires kept their shields held high, no arrow could penetrate their armor and no spells could confuse their minds. Garrett wrestled with the enticing thought to lower his shield just enough to catch a glimpse of the enemy. But when he saw another squire do it, only to have arrows whizzing by, he abandoned the thought. More thoughts drifted through his mind. The spells floated in and around the soldiers like a fog.

The more seasoned warriors raised their praise when some of the others began to weaken.

Sir Leo continued to call out to the men to stand strong. "We are on our way to rescue our brother who has been taken captive. Remember our mission, remember our King!"

Garrett's head cleared momentarily. Other suggestions soon returned to cause him to want to lower his shield.

Once again, Sir Leo reminded his men, "You are stronger than the enemy if you keep your shield of Faith held high. Do not engage in warfare with the Keltoi. Stay focused on our mission."

In the meantime, the sisters in the abbey carried out their own warfare. The dramatic sounds of drums pounding, and tambourines jingling and banging as the women's loud voices resonated throughout, creating an offensive attack in the atmosphere. They knew that this terrified the enemy.

Abbess Joan the Joyful proclaimed on behalf of the knight who had been captured. "Sir Knight, you are able to think clearly and stand against the lies of Asmo." She requested the celestial army to take their declarations to the knight so that Truth could penetrate the lies he had come to believe.

Many of the sisters in the abbey danced the ancient war dance; their movements creating a breakthrough for Sir Spencer that went along with Abbess Joan's proclamations. Sister Penelope, using the secret language, called upon Lord Perazim to thwart the enemy so that none of their weapons would harm any of the soldiers. She also asked for the celestial army of King Elyon to help the soldiers get through the attacks and ambushes of the enemy.

Lord Perazim's invisible presence overwhelmed Devynne. A sense of urgency to call upon King Elyon in the secret language compelled the young damsel to put down her hand-sewing.

"Sir Spencer is in trouble, and I must petition King Elyon on his behalf," she told herself.

Pacing back and forth, Devynne felt drawn to the music room. Her flute lay across the music stand, beckoning her to play. Picking up her instrument, Devynne blew a strong, forceful sound beginning a tune she had never heard before. Yes, the lady-in-waiting played, but it seemed as if another directed her fingers and the force of her breath. The music changed. Sometimes the melody sounded sweet, like a serenade, and then abruptly changed to a military cadence. The notes fluttered like flames or wind. All the while, Devynne sent silent requests from her heart to King Elyon. The music floated across the air through the atmosphere and into the spiritual realm.

Suddenly, the lifeless gray changed to a fiery red. Long flaming tongues of fire spewed toward Sir Spencer! Ducking behind a huge stalagmite, the knight only slightly singed, escaped certain death by the large reptilian dragon with glowing beady yellow eyes. The dragon hissed and made a terrifying sound resembling the noise of clashing brass.

The knight realized that he had left his weapons along with his horse in the camp of the Keltois. Being helpless without his weapons, Sir Spencer cowered just out of reach of the malevolent monster.

At the same time, the knight found himself changing from self-pity to anger. He wailed in fury at the memory of all the people who had ever betrayed him. He seethed with anger at the ones who had mistreated him in any way. He raged toward those who had not intervened on his behalf when they should have.

All the hatred and anger that the dragon breathed on the knight in the smoldering fumes made him cry out in anguish.

Galloping across the plain the soldiers stayed out of reach of the shooting arrows. The spells continued to float on the waves of the air sent to weaken each soldier's resolve to continue on with the mission.

The Keltoi sorcerer called forth the asmodai to terrify the warriors. Massive ghouls came storming out of the woods on ghostly black steeds billowing brimstone and fire.

The celestial army charged ahead of the mortal soldiers. Attacking the asmodai with their swords, the celestial warriors sliced the ghouls across the neck. Their heads flying off their bodies as the ghostly stallions puffed into a cloud of swirling air and vanished.

Sir Bruce continued to hold his banner high as he proclaimed, "The weapons of our warfare are for destroying the power of the asmodai!"

The soldiers continued to fight the Keltoi.

In spite of all the bluster and terror of the asmodai, they were no match for the soldiers who had Prince Sabaoth on their side.

While some of the celestial warriors fought the asmodai, others helped protect the mortal soldiers in the heat of battle by keeping the flaming arrows from reaching their mark. They also whispered words of truth into the ears of the troops to counteract the lies of the spells that floated around them.

A squad of knights stayed behind at a distance to fend off the continuing attacks so the rest could advance into the cave.

Arriving in an area of gnarly old shade trees, the troop came to a ridge of exposed rocks and tree trunks at the top of a hillside and dismounted. Looking over the ledge, Sir Leo slid on his feet down the dirt and gravelly side of the short decline to the barren ground below. The other knights followed after him. Sir Leo found the large hidden entrance behind the shrubbery that clung to the crest of the hill.

Garrett and Sekiah, along with the other squires, waited under branches of a large knotty oak to hold the horses and guard the extra weapons for the knights.

Sir Bruce gave the red flag to Sekiah to put away. The knight then took out the amber flag, so they would enter the dreadful caverns with the glory of King Elyon.

Shields raised and swords extended, Sir Leo motioned to go forward. Sir Bruce led the way carrying the banner. The bright light emanating from the banner lit the way for the soldiers. The swords of Truth pierced the bleakness, enabling the knights to move boldly.

Lady Isabelle, in the midst of giving lessons to Luke, noticed the peculiar music coming from the music room. The lessons came to an abrupt halt.

"Something is wrong with Garrett," Luke said.

"How do you know that?" the lady asked.

"My heart knows," the child replied.

"Then you must sing a battle song for him," answered Lady Isabelle.

Eventually, the distant thought penetrated the knight's dark rages: *"How do I get out of here?"* Perceiving that he now had thoughts of his own again, Sir Spencer remembered to call upon King Elyon for help. At the top of his lungs, with all the strength he could muster, the knight yelled, "I am a knight of King Elyon, and I call upon Prince Sabaoth to save me."

The sound of desperate faith penetrated into the celestial realm. King Elyon heard one of his own crying out to be rescued. The gladness in his heart overflowed into his feet and once again the Great King leapt rejoicing at another great triumph among his dear mortals.

At that very instant, the bright light radiating from the banner illuminated the cavern as the knights rounded the corner. The howling and hideous sounds ceased. The asmodai fled into the dark crevices. The startled bats flew away, and the beetles scurried into hiding.

The terrifying dragon, greedy to devour all the prey that had entered its den, billowed its fiercest smoke and burning fire as it bounded toward the soldiers.

Unafraid, Sir Leo charged forward with his sword lunging at the dragon, crying, "In the name of Prince Sabaoth I cut you down, foul beast!" His shield deflecting the effects of the spewing fire, Sir Leo plunged his sword into the dragon's scaly throat. The other knights joined the attack and thrust their blades into the screeching creature's elongated writhing neck and flailing leathery bat-like wings. Blood and smoke spewed from the fatal gashes. The once ferocious monster plummeted lifeless into the black depths of the cave.

The asmodai, frightened but not willing to surrender since they claimed the caverns as their rightful territory, regrouped themselves to resist the mortal knights. Some slithered out of the crevices, others crawled out from behind the rocks and began to shriek and holler. Others wailed and screamed or cried and moaned as if in horrible agony. The asmodai used the terrifying noises to frighten the soldiers. Even then, Sir Leo and his soldiers felt no intimidation. In fact, nothing the asmodai did worked to thwart their mission.

When it became apparent that the soldiers would not be turned back, a monstrous creature emerged from the blackness. With evil in its dark voice and hatred in its green, misshapen eyes, the asmode proudly boasted of its might. "No mere mortal can stand against me! I have supernatural powers beyond your miniscule strength!"

"We do not come in our own power," Sir Leo answered undaunted. "We come in the name of Prince Sabaoth!" the knight announced.

"AAAAGH!" cried the grotesque asmode. Vapors emitted forth from the huge black creature. The fumes became a nauseous stench. Gasping and clawing at the air, the creature began to shrink until it became the size of a bug. Sir Leo could easily step on it. So he did.

This time the asmodai, large and small, could not withstand the soldiers. Once again the shrieks and wails echoed throughout the cave as they slithered and crawled back into the furthest recesses of the caverns.

Sir Tyler went over to Sir Spencer to help him up.

"I have discarded my horse and weapons," bemoaned Sir Spencer to his comrade.

"We shall find a way to retrieve them." Sir Tyler replied.

Though weak from the ordeal and burned from the scorching flames of the dragon, Sir Spencer walked out on his own.

Sir Bruce led the way holding the brilliantly glowing amber banner through the chambers as they departed the Caverns of Cataclysmic Calamities.

The Dark and Stormy Night

Chapter 10

Stepping out of the cave into the fresh air, the cool evening breeze helped to revive the knights. Sir Spencer collapsed on the grassy slope above the opening of the cave, exhausted from the terrible ordeal he had just come through.

The Keltois had not let up their attack. The knights continued to repel the flaming arrows soaring through the air. The squires kept their post by the horses and weapons. Some took replacement weapons to the knights on the battlefield.

Garrett had sustained a hit in the leg and sat propped up against a broad elm tree near Valiant. Sekiah attended him as best he could until a knight could take charge. The young squire sat quietly moaning against the tree as Sekiah talked softly to distract him from the pain.

With a whimper, the young squire asked his friend, "Sekiah, will I ever do my war dance again? Will I even walk normal?"

"I'm sure you will be all right," Sekiah said. "You are in a lot of pain right now, but once you get well, you will dance like before. Besides, I need you to dance when I waive my banners."

"Not on the battlefield with mortals, though!" Garrett said.

Sir Leo came over and bent down to get a look at Garrett's leg. The knight asked Sekiah if he knew what had happened.

"We were standing near each other with our shields up when I looked over and saw him set his shield down." Sekiah answered pointing to the area where they had been stationed. "Garrett saw me and said that his shield was heavy and he wanted to rest for just a minute. He seemed to be listening to the voices whispering in the breeze that we are not to pay attention to and then the arrow got him."

"Bruce!" Sir Leo called. "Hold the squire down while I pull the shaft off." Since the shaft was attached to the arrowhead by beeswax, it came off with relative ease; however, any movement at the site of the wound did not feel gentle to Garrett! Although brave for a lad his age, Garrett could not stop himself from crying out as the warrior worked on removing the shaft. Sekiah stood by softly asking King Elyon to help his friend recover from the injury quickly. Sir Bruce wrapped a tourniquet around the wound to keep the blood from gushing. Garrett lay motionless on the grassy slope near Sir Spencer, passed-out from the trauma.

Sir Leo called Sir Walter over to be apart of the discussion with Sir Bruce regarding their next move. Sizing up the situation, they decided that splitting into two groups would give them the best advantage for getting back safely.

"You and I will take the group with the wounded," Sir Leo decided. "We'll take the long way around going behind the Keltois on the other side of the woods and then head toward the abbey. At the same time, have Sir Ellison take the rest of the soldiers to distract the Keltoi before dashing across the plain back to the outpost. I want you to come with me so we can assist the sisters with the wounded."

"We must also retrieve Sir Spencer's horse and weapons," said Sir Walter.

"Yes," replied Sir Leo. "He cannot continue without them. Take what troops you need and bring the young knight's horse and weapons to the abbey."

As Sir Ellison and his troops shot arrows into the trees above the Keltois, the Keltois finally began to grow weary. They could not understand why their arrows missed their marks or the incantations and spells had no effect. The Keltois also did not realize that not all the soldiers crossed the field together. When Sir Ellison knew that the other group had reached the safety of the far side of the woods, his soldiers retreated across the field back to the outpost.

Sir Leo held onto Garrett to keep him propped up as they slowly rode toward the abbey. The unit took their time in order to prevent any undo pain to the squire, and watched out for Sir Spencer, who still lacked strength.

Sir Walter took Sir Tyler and both their squires stealthily into the thick of the forest to the outskirts of the Keltoi's camp. Mostly abandoned, only the old grandmothers watched over the young children. The soldiers spied Sir Spencer's horse grazing nearby along with the other tethered horses of the Keltoi.

"Sir Tyler," directed Sir Walter. "You and your squire take the horse while we cover you."

Riding boldly into the camp, Sekiah dismounted and untethered the horse. Hastily, he remounted Judah while holding onto the reigns of Sir Spencer's horse.

"Look!" one of the children cried in alarm. "Soldiers are stealing our horses!"

Before any in the camp could get help to stop them, the troop dashed out of the woods and with all due haste safely crossed the plain.

Riding on ahead of the others, Sekiah drew out the blue banner from its holder and waved it to signal the abbey that they would be bringing in wounded. Upon seeing the flag flying at the squire's approach, the sister keeping watch from the tower informed the abbess. Abbess Joan beckoned Sister Mary Elizabeth to go to the village below to bring the widow Robynne. A devout woman, she provided much needed care to the sick through the use of herbs to produce homemade medicines and potions. The sister quickly fetched her cloak and lantern on her way out of the abbey. The setting sun began to usher in the fast approaching dusk.

Walking through the village consisting of a cluster of hovels made of woven twigs plastered with mud to form a hard wall, called wattle and daub, the sister came to the widow's door.

"Hello!" called out Sister Mary Elizabeth upon entering the cottage. Finding the 'wise woman' working in her kitchen making tinctures, oils and ointments, she watched as the widow ladled out the rest of the herbal solution from her caldron.

"Welcome sister!" Robynne cheerfully acknowledged. The pungent aromas permeated the air. A mixture brewed in her caldron over the coals while a different tincture cooled in bottles on the table.

"I so enjoy coming to your house," Sister Mary Elizabeth enthused. "All the fragrances smell so unusual, and your work is quite interesting."

"You know," said Robynne, "I still find my work fascinating, and I've been doing it a good many years.

"Did your mother or grandmother pass on her knowledge to you?" asked the sister inquisitively.

"My older brother did," Robynne answered, pleased to talk about him. "Grayson studied under the Benedictines at the University of Salerno. Many a year ago, when I was a youth, he returned for a long visit. While he was here, Grayson taught me all he knew. It has helped greatly to provide for my children and myself when I became widowed. My brother made this plaque above the mantle for me," she said, pointing to a beautiful inscription carved in wood.

"Learn, therefore, the nature of herbs, and study diligently the way to combine their various species for human health. But do not place your entire hope on herbs, nor seek to restore health only by human counsels. Since medicine has been created by King Elyon, and since it is he who gives back health and restores life, turn to him...." Cassiodorus (468-560 a.d.).

"Well now, I know you, sister," Robynne stated matter of factly. "You did not come here just to watch me make concoctions. How may I be of service to you?"

"We need you at the abbey," replied Sister Mary Elizabeth. Then the sister proceeded to tell the wise woman about the wounded soldiers and asked her to come.

Robynne called to her devoted daughter Tahlor, to assist her in gathering together the medicinal salves and liniments she would need.

"Jordie," Robynne called to her young son. "Hold the basket for me while I pick some herbs from the garden. I'll only be gone overnight," she instructed both children, "so I need you two to tend the gardens and care for the animals for me tomorrow."

Grabbing up her cloak and kissing her children in parting, the two women walked quickly together in the twilight up the hill toward the abbey. The brisk wind blew their cloaks all around making it difficult for the ladies not to become tripped up in their garments.

The moon played hide and seek behind the clouds, casting eerie shadows on the ground. Gusts of wind prevented their lanterns from holding steady.

Tahlor and Jordie watched out the doorway as the two lanterns, swaying in the dusk, grew smaller in the distance. Already full of trepidation at the darkening sky with menacing clouds and wild wind, the children, now overcome with terror from the sudden crash of thunder, screamed. Tahlor grabbed a lantern from the table as they both ran into the night after their mother and the sister. Each of them hollered into the darkness, but the wind carried off their cries, unheard by the women fading into the blackness.

From the abbey window, Sir Bruce saw the change in the sky. He knew the climb up the hill to the abbey would be difficult for the ladies in this weather, so the knight gestured to Sekiah to come with him as he went after Sister Mary Elizabeth and the widow, Robynne. Descending the hill toward the village, the fierce wind caught the two off guard by blowing against them one minute; trying its best to push them backward the next, and then swirling around to thrust them forward. The sound of thunder rumbling in the distance warned them of the impending storm fast approaching.

The buffeting winds made it grueling to try and run or even walk. Tahlor wondered if they could ever catch up. Lightning zig-zagged across the sky with blinding streaks that terrified the children. Great drops of rain pelted down soaking them to the skin.

"We're going to die, Tahlor," sobbed Jordie.

"Don't talk like that or Asmo will hear you and then we *will* die!" yelled his sister. Miserable and frightened, Tahlor knew they could not go on anymore. "King Elyon!" she screamed, "Help us!"

"Yes," echoed Jordie. "Send your celestial warriors to bring someone to help us!"

Sir Bruce and Sekiah hurried their pace when they saw the lightning shatter across the sky. Rain would soon follow. They reached the women just as the sky let forth a great downpour. In practically no time the foursome entered the safety of the abbey.

Sir Tyler watched out the window as Sir Bruce and Sekiah left the abbey, glad that he had not been called upon to venture out into the storm. He saw the swaying lanterns of the ladies fighting their way up the hill through the wind. Further down the path, a speck of light caught his eye. The woods allowed him to catch only glimpses of it. The light struggled to climb the hill as it staggered back and forth. Sir Tyler knew that he had to go help the mortal making such little progress with so much effort.

Flinging his cloak around himself, Sir Tyler grabbed his lantern. In haste to reach the struggling mortal, the knight startled the soaking wet party that had just arrived inside the refuge of the abbey as he rushed by on his way out into the dark and stormy night.

Quickly taking off her cloak and briefly warming herself by the fire, the widow immediately took charge by giving orders to one sister to boil some water, to another to get clean cloths.

"Sir Bruce," she directed, "I want you to hold Garrett down while Sir Leo helps me extract the arrowhead from his leg. Sister Penelope, please stay nearby in case I need your assistance. Sister Mary Elizabeth, remain close to the door so you can bring me fresh towels and more hot water, if I need it."

At the very moment Tahlor and Jordie could no longer take even one more step in front of the other, a large ominous figure with a bright lantern came upon them. They had not seen the light moving toward them as the two had kept their heads down in the fierce storm. The light from the lantern cast frightening shadows across Sir Tyler's face.

Alarmed, both children shrieked in terror. Covering their heads in fear at the mysteriously cloaked figure, Tahlor and Jordie knew for sure that Asmo himself had come to take them down to the caverns!

Above the noise of the wind and pelting rain, the children heard a reassuring voice. "I am Sir Tyler," the knight said to them. "I saw your lantern from the abbey and came down to assist you the rest of the way." To calm the children, the knight threw back his hood and squatted down with his lantern next to his face to let them see him better.

Tahlor and Jordie remembered their panicked cry to King Elyon for help. "King Elyon sent you!" shouted Jordie.

Though the knight did not understand the boy's meaning, he felt pleased to come in response to the child's cry.

The rest of the journey seemed less difficult now that Sir Tyler accompanied them. He carried Jordie in one arm and grasped Tahlor's hand with his other, pulling her along against the wiles of the wind.

Resting by the fire after tending to the sick and wounded, the soldiers and women sipped their soothing hot tea and quietly talked with each other. Abruptly, the quiet atmosphere changed to astonishment as the sopping wet trio arrived safely inside the abbey. The most astonished of all, the widow Robynne thought her children lay safely tucked in their own beds!

Stay at the Abbey

Chapter 11

The welcoming fire loudly snapped and popped in the large stone fireplace. Bright embers glowed orangey-red under the burning black logs. The thick grey smoke rolled and curled its way up the chimney as sparks chased each other to the top. Tahlor and Jordie sat on either side of their mother in a large worn chair near the hearth warming themselves. With great drama, they told about their terrible ordeal. Robynne listened, grateful that her precious children were safe beside her inside the abbey where only the sound of the whistling and moaning wind could penetrate.

"That wind was so strong I started to blow away into the sky, but Tahlor grabbed hold of me just as my feet went off the ground!" Jordie said, flailing his arms about like the wind.

"You did not!" scolded Tahlor. "You are exaggerating."

"Perhaps the young lad remembers the terrors of the climb differently than you," suggested Sister Penelope as she entered the room.

"I did too!" argued Jordie. "I also nearly got struck with lightning, too. And, Asmo came to take us away but that turned out to be Sir Tyler."

"Well," laughed Robynne. "At least you remember something the way it actually happened."

"Yeh," agreed Jordie. "But my story is more interesting than the way Tahlor told it."

"Not that it needed any embellishing," said Sir Bruce. "But it was definitely entertaining."

"That's the way I like to tell a story," Jordie replied, looking over at his sister.

Everyone chuckled.

Sir Leo met the sister carrying an ample tray full of cups and a generous kettle with steaming hot water for tea.

"Let me help you with that," he said, taking the heavy tray and setting it down. As the sister poured out, Sir Leo took the cups and handed them around to each one in the room.

Sipping their warm chamomile tea calmed their frayed nerves and relaxed their tired bodies. Pretty soon everyone began to feel drowsy. Jordie set his cup down on the small table near the chair and climbed into his mother's lap. Cradling her mug in both hands, Tahlor rested her head on her mother's shoulder as she let out a great yawn. Robynne became conscious of how exceedingly tired she felt as well as she tried to stifle her own yawn.

"Merciful heavens, children!" Abbess Joan exclaimed, setting down her teacup and rising from her chair on the far side of the fireplace. She laughed apologetically, "How thoughtless of me not to see how worn out your awful experience has made you! Follow me as I take you to your room." Turning back, she addressed the knights and squires. "Sister Penelope will show you to your rooms down that corridor," the abbess said. She pointed toward a long hallway lit by candles placed in sconces and the occasional flash of lightning coming through the tall windows. "Sleep well, gentlemen. Sir Tyler, since Garrett is your squire you may keep watch in his room tonight."

Then walking over to the elderly sister, the abbess addressed the weary woman in her gentle manner. "Sister Mary Elizabeth, go onto your own room, now. You have had quite a day making that arduous walk in the storm and then helping our dear friend Robynne with the young soldiers," she said kindly. "You've had plenty of vigorous activity for one evening."

The abbey grew quiet as all the inhabitants settled down for the night, safe from the raging storm outside. A special tonic given to Sir Spencer made him sleep in peaceful slumber.

Garrett, however, grew feverish in the night and became delirious by the infection from his wound. Crying out in anguish, Garrett's mind tormented him as he relived the moments that surrounded getting hit by the arrow. He had his shield raised, and he stood at his post. But it was taking too long for the others to return with Sir Spencer, and he began to grow weary. If he could just set his shield down for a moment...."Agh!" he screamed, experiencing the moment again when the arrow struck.

Sir Tyler jumped out of his bed, alarmed. Trying to waken themselves, the sisters and widow stumbled through their doors into the hallway, pulling their robes about them. The abbess opened Garrett's door to find Sir Tyler already putting wet cloths on the squire's forehead to reduce his fever. She heard the knight beseeching King Elyon on Garrett's behalf.

Following behind Abbess Joan, the widow Robynne calmly went over to the bedside next to Sir Tyler.

"You are tending to our young soldier quite nicely," she affirmed. "Allow me to take charge, now, if you will."

"Gladly, ma'am," said Sir Tyler, stepping aside. "He keeps crying out that he will never dance again."

The widow assessed the condition of Garrett's wound and fever. "As long as the infection does not go into gangrene, he will dance again. However, his wound is deep and it will take considerable time to heal. I would not be too concerned about gangrene since we were able to attend to his injury rather quickly," stated the widow, matter-of-factly.

Sir Tyler sat watching as Sister Penelope assisted Robynne. Abbess Joan earnestly spoke to King Elyon in the secret language in the hallway. Garrett finally lay quietly sleeping.

At last the long eventful night gave way to the gray light of dawn. Morning brought with it clear skies and crisp clean air washed by the nights' rainstorm. Sir Tyler went to check on his friend, Sir Spencer. He found the young knight lying on his bed recalling how he had allowed himself to be captured by the asmodai.

"By neglecting to suit up in my spiritual armour yesterday," he said out loud to himself, "I listened to the deceptive words of the chieftain's flattery. That caused me to let down my guard and be overcome by the asmodai."

Sir Tyler went over to sit in the chair by Sir Spencer's bed, and listened to his comrade's confession.

"I repent to Prince Sabaoth for neglecting to put on my armour!" exclaimed Sir Spencer, tears rolling down his cheeks. (Knights do not usually cry, for it is not considered very knightly. However, there are occasions when it is most appropriate to express emotions through tears. Repentance is one of those times.)

"Let me remind you Spencer, that when we ask Prince Sabaoth to forgive us for doing the wrong thing, or neglecting to do the right thing, we give him the ability to heal our souls by taking the pain out of our hearts."

Commissioned from the throne room, the celestial emissaries not only mysteriously tended to Garrett, but they also cared for Sir Spencer. The wounded and the weak spent the day quietly resting and recovering. Garrett's fever broke, and he too felt at peace after asking Prince Sabaoth to forgive him for setting down his shield. It would take at least another day before the party could travel again.

The Tale

After breakfast, the abbess led morning service. Standing in front of the little congregation, she scanned the room filled with knights and nuns. She began.

"Let me tell you a little tale. I will tell you how I became known as 'Joan the Joyful'. I did not start out that way," the abbess said with a great laugh. "Oh, no! It took me many years before I experienced the constant joy that Lord Perazim bestows upon those who are obedient to forgive and repent. Joy is the balm he applies when he heals their broken hearts. But I will start from the very beginning so that you will understand why I did not have it to begin with.

"I was born the daughter of a very wealthy Baron. Even as a young child I had my own little pony to ride and my own servants to order about. I was a very privileged child," exclaimed the Abbess throwing her head back in a hearty fit of laughter. "I lived in privilege until the day a stranger came to the door of the manor house of the grand estate seeking employment.

"I had been told never to open the door. Only servants were allowed to. But that day, none of the servants came to the door. Instead of being obedient and looking for a servant, I opened it myself. The stranger, upon seeing my long curly red hair and lively manner thought I must be an exquisite doll come to life!

"So, instead of asking for work, he took me away right then to give to his wife, who could not have children. At first, I thought I was only there to visit and to cheer her. She treated me kindly until I asked to go home again. Flying into a fit of rage, the wife insisted I call her 'mum,' and she punished me when I did not please her, which was most of the time. Being of noble birth, I did not know how to tend to household chores or other duties of peasant life!" With that, the Abbess nearly doubled over in laughter.

"I often dreamed that the Baron and Baroness came looking for me, and I'm sure that they did. But the peasants who kidnapped me moved far away so I would not be found. I grew very thin. My beautiful red hair became dirty, and my pretty dress got all tattered and torn. It was my only dress, even when it became too small. I was not joyful at all," she said, interrupting herself with another fit of laughter.

"Over time I made a plan to escape. I was determined to somehow find my way back to my family and the life I had known before. I set out one night when I was about thirteen. Furtively, I crept out into the dark in the wee small hours of the night when the dogs would not hearken to bark. It was a dark night with no moon. The distant sounds of animals calling out to each other terrified me. I had heard of vicious foxes and wild boars as well as dragons that also came out of their dens on these moonless nights. I was deathly afraid of bats and imagined that they were vicious vampires stationed in the low limbs of the trees just waiting for me to leave the hovel. But I was more determined to escape the beatings and abuse of my captors than I was afraid of the terrors in the night. I did not stop until late the next day when I met a band of Keltois, just like the one that Sir Spencer and his companions encountered yesterday," the abbess said, nodding toward the knights and squire.

"The chieftain invited me to join them, so I did. In the beginning, everyone was so kind and caring toward me. The older women acted like mothers and the younger girls treated me like a sister, so I stayed with the caravan for several years. The women taught me the secrets of their black magic, and after much practice I could eventually cast spells and do all manner of incantations. It was exciting and fun," Abbess Joan said in all seriousness. "Oh yes! The occult is very intriguing. I had tapped into a mighty power that gave me a sense of control. I found the study of astrology to be quite fascinating and even came to the belief that the alignment and movements of the sun, moon and other planets affects mortals. During that phase of my training, the Keltois also taught me how to read horoscopes and tell others their future by gazing into a crystal ball.

"When we came to a town, we strode through the main street advertising our faire which we had set up in a field nearby with colorful tents adorned with streamers and flags. We used the tents to hold private sessions with paying customers to tell them their future and conduct séances.

"Many came with questions that we answered with the help of the asmodai. They were so amazed that we could tell them specific details about their lives that a stranger could not possibly know. We earned lots of money this way.

"In the open air, the menfolk and boys would entertain the townsfolk with sorcery. They marveled at the thrilling displays of the supernatural. The peasants were easily taken in by the flashy and impossible feats performed by mere mortals. Our spectacular shows brought us fame and renown.

"Then one day near a village where we were performing, a monk came to our carnival. He paid me to sit at my table. But, instead of asking me to read his fortune, he gazed directly into my eyes with a piercing stare. He saw right into my soul! I was frightened, but he told me about Prince Sabaoth and his sacrifice for my life and that by being in league with Asmo, I had become a traitor to King Elyon.

"This monk told me that when we conduct séances, the spirit of the dead is not really speaking to us, but an asmode posing as the dead person. He told me that horoscopes are connected with astrology and is used to manipulate and deceive mortals; that talking with the dead is forbidden by King Elyon and is called necromancy.

"Well!" exclaimed the abbess, as she looked at the faces riveted in front of her. "I was so shocked to hear his words, but something inside me wondered if he indeed spoke the truth.

"This monk said that he would do spiritual warfare for me until the battle between King Elyon and Asmo had been won in my mortal soul. Warfare was the only way for me to escape the slavery I was in. However, I could not yet see for myself that I was in bondage. I had seen the powers of Asmo and what his minions could do through the Keltois, and I felt as though King Elyon was no match for the Keltois' powers. I had not seen any battles between the two forces or heard of any great feats this King Elyon had performed. What I saw I believed to be evidence of Asmo's mighty power. I did not understand then that what I witnessed was merely the residue that was left after he lost his splendor when he was defeated in the Great Cosmic War.

"For a while, I was content to be a part of the caravan because they made me feel that I was a part of a family, and it had been a long time since I had ever felt that I belonged anywhere," the abbess continued. "Over time there came a gradual change. The more dedicated I became to learning the arts and rituals of witchcraft, the more I lost connection with my own self. I also noticed that each of us seemed to be losing control over the forces we called upon. Instead, we began to get swept along by forces beyond our command. Asmodai are highly intelligent dark spiritual forces of evil whose intent is to destroy all their followers.

"The mind games that some of the others, especially the wife of the chieftain, played on me were all designed to break me down mentally. The spirits that worked through the Keltois exercised mind control that eventually reduced me to a shuffling zombie because of the many sleepless nights being tormented by the relentless assault. I knew that they would not just let me leave, so I had to devise a plan of escape. This was worse than fleeing my first captors!

"In time, our wanderings led us to a town at the bottom of an immense hill. On top of this hill stood the most beautiful castle I had ever seen! It looked the way I would imagine heaven to be. It was enormous. We had no knowledge that King Waymon would not tolerate the kinds of faires and carnivals that we held in many villages. On the day we arrived, the sheriff informed us that because it was late in the afternoon, we could only camp nearby for the night and move on the next morning. Appearing agreeable, we made camp that evening. However, while we set up our camp, we cast spells on the town. The next morning, our chieftain took several men with him to speak with the sheriff about allowing us to entertain the inhabitants that day. He was confident the spells they had cast the previous evening would do their magick to change the sheriff's disposition toward us. However, unbeknownst to them, the sheriff had already called upon the castle to send some soldiers to rid us off the king's land entirely. He had previous experience with other caravans like ours. It was the only time that our spells had no effect.

"As the king's knights drove us from the woods, I saw my opportunity to escape. There before me was a knight in shining armour, and yes – he was riding a pure white stallion!" With

- 125 -

that, Abbess Joan burst out with a great guffaw. "I ran as fast as I could toward him and begged him to rescue me from the troupe. He pulled me up onto his steed, and we galloped back to the castle.

"The most amazing part of my story is that when I renounced my loyalty to Asmo and pledged my allegiance to King Elyon, I felt as though I had finally found what I had been looking for all my life!

"I remembered the words that the monk had spoken to me months earlier and realized that they were in fact true!" Abbess Joan said with great passion.

"The castle where the knight took me was filled with people who were busy working diligently. They were happy, and they liked their work. They even liked each other!" she threw her head back again in hysterics. "This is where I learned that Prince Sabaoth has authority and power with grace and love to help mortals heal from their wounded emotions. Prince Sabaoth has continued to heal me. At first it was dramatic, but over the years I have felt Prince Sabaoth heal me in more subtle ways. I am also aware of him continually changing my heart. He could have stopped when he brought his healing, but he also put laughter in my soul! Hallelujah!" cried Abbess Joan. "Now you know my story and why the title, 'Joan the Joyful' was bestowed upon me."

When the chapel service concluded, Sir Bruce invited Sekiah to join him for a ride in the countryside. The squire eagerly accepted the welcome offer. Coming down the sloping hill still wet from the night's storm, they met up with the widow and her children returning home. After exchanging greetings with one another, the two on horseback quickened their pace along the winding path. Sekiah felt invigorated as he listened to the birds chirping on this splendid day.

Glad for this time alone with Sir Bruce, Sekiah took the opportunity to ask the knight about many things.

"Sir Bruce," Sekiah inquired. "Was that the only dragon in the caverns?"

"No," replied the knight. "There are many dragons down there, and there are many more dragon eggs. We only fight them when we have to."

"I have heard many stories about the caverns," said Sekiah. "But I have never known anyone who actually went into them. What were they like? Were you afraid to go down?"

"I was not afraid," answered Sir Bruce. "I had the glory of King Elyon with me. The banner lit up the caverns so we could see all around as if it were daylight. Only the asmodai were afraid!" Sir Bruce said smiling as he recalled to Sekiah how Sir Leo had stood up against them.

The conversation changed to other matters until Sir Bruce became weary of answering so many questions from the inquisitive squire.

"How about a race?" he said, nudging his horse Banner, to gallop.

Sekiah leaned into Judah who took off at a full run out into the open meadow. The surging energy of his horse and fresh air whooshing past his face thrilled the lad.

Bamboozled!

Chapter 12

Garrett's fever left. The previous day spent in bed did much to return a good deal of the youth's strength and vigor. His leg, however, would require further care for some time while it slowly mended.

Sir Spencer felt fully restored. His slight burns healing under the soothing liniment. A hard lesson learned now fortified the young soldier against neglecting his invisible armour.

As the knights prepared for their departure, Sir Leo found them in the stables with their horses.

"Top of the morn, lads!" he greeted in his jovial way. "After such adventure as you young soldiers have already encountered, I trust the rest of your journey shall be uneventful. Midway to the castle you will arrive at a town called Brookshire. You will come to it after a long morning's ride. The abbess tells me that the peasants have turned away from King Elyon. I say this so you will be prepared for the dark mood of the town."

Thanking the knight for his help and counsel, the troop set out from Beste Abbey with gratefulness in their hearts for the sisters of the abbey and the warriors from the fortress. Sekiah unfurled the green banner, rejoicing in the new beginning of this fresh day.

The morning sun struggled to break through the haze. While the horses plodded up the hillside, the riders thrilled at the breathtaking view of the morning mist rising from the valley below. A shimmering lake twinkled as if stars danced on it. Bluebells and yellow daffodils dotted the trail. The white wood anemone growing in profusion blanketed the ground causing it to appear as if covered with a late spring snow. The cry of a lark broke the monotonous sound of the horses' hooves climbing the path before them. Sekiah could not help but break into song.

"All right, Sekiah!" exclaimed Sir Tyler in mock exasperation. "If you must insist on making the birds fly away in fright, then we all might as well warble along with you!" This time the others joined him.

A flash of light sparkled in the heather. *"Was that the sound of a child's laughter? Too many faerie tales; or is it a faerie? What just dashed behind that stump?"* Garrett thought he saw the backside of a gnome.

"Sekiah!" loudly whispered Garrett. "Did you see that?"

"What?" asked Sekiah.

"That!" Garrett said as softly as he could, pointing in the direction of another flicker.

"What is it?" Sekiah asked, astonished.

"I don't know," replied Garrett.

Sir Spencer and Sir Tyler had also seen the strange glint in the woods. Sometimes it looked as if the sparks of light were playing hide and seek with each other. Some appeared to be dancing.

It began to dawn on Garrett first. "We must be coming upon a borough for faeries and pixies and other-worldly creatures, not mortal," he said. "I have heard that these beings have magickal abilities and powers and are often quite beautiful to look at."

Sir Spencer heard Lord Perazim advise him to be cautious. He told the group to make sure they had on their full armor of protection against the unseen enemy. Sekiah put away the green flag and opened the black one, for he remembered they were coming into a place of spiritual darkness.

"In the name of Prince Sabaoth," Sir Spencer pronounced, "Buckle on the belt of Truth. Put on the breastplate of Righteousness. Lace on the shoes of readiness to proclaim the good news of Peace. Strap on the shield of Faith to put out all the flaming arrows of the invisible enemy. Wear the helmet of Deliverance and wield the sword which is the Sacred Scroll. Send messages to King Elyon, using the secret language; be always vigilant and persistent on behalf of all the King's subjects."

Coming into a clearing on the far side of the hill, the town of Brookshire came into view. The farmers seen toiling in the fields had the spring planting well underway.

The soldiers reached Brookshire around noontime. Standing outside the stables and talking with the stable hand, the sheriff saw the knights and their squires riding into town. It being his duty to greet them, he introduced himself to the soldiers and asked their business.

"We are on our way to Brighton Castle," Sir Spencer answered.

Again! More flashes of light! This time they played peek-a-boo behind the sheriff. Garrett and Sekiah became distracted by the flickering of the faeries. They looked so cute, appearing sweet and harmless. A little girl came up to Sheriff Festus, who introduced her to the soldiers.

"This is my daughter, Asceline," he proudly boasted. She looked about three years old.

"What did she hold in her leather pouch?" Sekiah wondered.

The moving lump stuck part way out, shimmering like the other lights.

"What have you there wee one?" inquired Sir Tyler. In response, the child hugged the bulging purse a little closer to herself.

"'Tis one of the pixies come to play with her," the sheriff stated. "Come dine with us," Sheriff Festus invited. "My wife can add more to the broth to make ample stew for whomever I happen to bring home."

The riders accepted. The soldiers dismounted to walk with their host, except for Garrett who did not want to limp very far. Upon learning of the injury Garrett sustained, Sheriff Festus offered to send for Petronilla, the 'wise woman' in the village who made healing poultices.

"She has learned the mysteries of how to live in peace and harmony with the universe," the sheriff said with a tone of admiration. "Petronilla uses her magick to cure the sick and injured. She does midwifery and knows the secrets of the earth for healing," explained the sheriff. "She even gets counsel from the faeries who teach her folk magick when she makes her potions. Since Petronilla arrived, more and more of the faeries and pixies have made their presence known. They have to be invited, you know, because they're rather shy at first."

"Is this similar to the witchcraft that the Keltois practice?" Sekiah asked.

"Oh no, young squire!" Sheriff Festus quickly answered, with a defensive tone in his voice at the suggestion. "Petronilla is a folk witch and only practices white magick for good purposes or to counteract evil. The Keltois are an evil band of mortals who use their black magick for harm. Petronilla is a faerie witch from the land of Northvegia," The sheriff replied. "The faerie sprites came with her. She was part of a Viking settlement that was attacked by knights a few years ago," the sheriff continued. "While Petronilla was in the woods, the knights destroyed her village. She could only flee before they spied her. Petronilla found her way to our town. On rare occasions they just come to play, as they are doing now." Sheriff Festus stated keenly. "Also, they come out from time to time to impart to her their wisdom and knowledge.

"Today would be an ideal opportunity for Petronilla to look at your wound," Sheriff Festus said to Garrett. Especially with the added aid of the faerie sprites available to her," he said in his most persuasive tone.

It proved to be a difficult task in Convincing the sheriff that Garrett had already been attended to by a woman of great skill.

As the group walked unhurriedly toward the sheriff's house, they observed a young woman crying on her way to fill her bucket at the town well.

Seeing the concerned looks on the visitor's faces, Sheriff Festus explained. "That is Christiana; she is the woman who speaks to her imaginary King Elyon. No faeries or pixies ever fly around that fanatical woman!" the sheriff said with scorn. "They dislike her very much."

Believing they did not understand his brief explanation, Sheriff Festus elaborated with disdain in his voice. "She speaks to her celestial king against the faerie sprites. But we do not believe in such a King as we once did. Christiana also warns us concerning a spirit called Asmo; but we do not believe in Asmo, either. Most of the mortals here think she is slightly peculiar. That maiden can be very persuasive and has convinced some to believe in King Elyon again."

With an air of patronizing benevolence, Sheriff Festus boasted, "Petronilla tried to persuade me to have her burned at the stake. I won't do it because although she is strange, I know she is not a witch and should not receive a witch's sentence."

Sheriff Festus continued. "Christiana blames the tragedies that happened here recently on Asmo. She calls upon her King Elyon to stop the bad things that are taking place. She believes that all the tragedies come from Asmo and his minions she calls asmodai. We only have faeries and pixies. They are helpful and friendly and cause us no harm."

"What tragedies?" Garrett asked.

Looking up at the young squire on his horse, then at the others walking in the group, the sheriff spoke as if betraying a confidence. "Some of the youth have been learning folk magick from Petronilla. She teaches them a strong moral code of which the parents approve. She shows them how they can come into peace and harmony with the universe the way she does, so they can summon the powers of nature and the sprites for themselves.

"Petronilla has also been teaching some of the young mortals, who have been doing this longer, how to perform 'protection magick' to ward off 'harmful voices' in their heads. These youths must not be practicing their magick correctly. It is tragic that some of these children of good parents have either killed themselves or gone insane," finished the sheriff.

Christiana overheard the discourse the sheriff held with the soldiers as she lowered her bucket into the well. Filling the pail, the maiden turned the crank to draw the bucket back up. Christiana gazed at the strangers passing by. As she hoisted the heavy pail onto the stone wall of the well, the young peasant woman released the hook attached to the rope from the handle. Lifting the pail off the wall, she spied the rolled-up banners sticking out of their holder on the back of Sekiah's horse, and especially noted the black flag unfurled. Drying her eyes, she approached the soldiers.

"I beg your pardons, sirs," the maiden said. "I see your colorful banners. Prince Sabaoth has sent you to come by this way. His purposes will be accomplished in Brookshire," Christiana said with relief in her voice. With that, the maiden abruptly turned, picked up her bucket, and went home.

Dismissing the interruption, Sheriff Festus suggested that they pay no attention to the "ramblings of a lunatic," as he called her.

"Because she talks to King Elyon?" exclaimed Sir Tyler.

"She causes no harm," the sheriff said with disdain.

The group arrived at the sheriff's simple wattle and daub dwelling toward the center of the village. His cordial wife Maerwynn welcomed all into their homely cottage sparsely furnished with crude wooden table, benches and chair. Even the eating implements were hand carved. The bed in the corner provided a soft spot for the sleeping cat. The smoldering fire took the slight chill out of the cool air of the dark interior. The savory smells of freshly baked rye bread cooling on the table along with the turnip and leek stew simmering in the pot over the fire drew the hungry lads toward the dining table. Sitting down, the conversation changed to more general topics which included the constant interruptions of delightful Asceline and her baby brother.

After asking about Garrett's injury, Maerwynn tried to sway the knights to take him to Petronilla.

"I have already made the offer, wife," Sheriff Festus informed her. "But they have refused my recommendation."

As the midday meal finished, the conversation turned back to the topic of Petronilla and Christiana.

"How did the whole town turn away from King Elyon to follow Petronilla?" Sir Tyler asked.

The sheriff, a bit reluctant to return to the previous discussion, rose from the table to indicate to his guests that it was time for them to be on their way. While expressing their hearty thanks to the sheriff's wife for her gracious hospitality and plentiful stew, the sheriff escorted the young soldiers back out into the light of day. The group returned for their horses tethered at the post nearby the sheriff's house.

"To give thee answer," said Sheriff Festus seething. "We followed all the laws King Elyon decreed. We diligently read the Holy Scroll, and we presented our requests to Him. We tried to love an unseen King, but finally it seemed to we mere mortals that there must not be any King in Britanniae besides King Waymon. He is king enough!" the sheriff said with disgust. "We witnessed no such power such as portrayed in the Holy Scroll."

"King Elyon has great power," said Sir Spencer, "but only for those who want to be his friend and not just obey him like servants."

"A king who wants his subjects for his friends?!" the sheriff exploded with incredulity.

"Yes," Sir Tyler said earnestly. "That is why He made mortals. But Asmo hates mortals and is jealous of us, so he works his wiles to cause us to believe in him instead."

"You speak as Christiana," the sheriff said, spewing the words out. "Her parents were overly devoted to King Elyon and she is even more so, if that is possible. Christiana has only caused trouble to the 'wise woman' who has brought a lot of good to our village. Even when the tragedies began, she used her magick to help us soothe our grief."

Garrett finally spoke up. "Sheriff, the pixies are like celestial beings of light, but they are not sweet and harmless, they are the asmodai in disguise!"

Sheriff Festus laughed at Garrett, "How can you prove that, young squire?"

"I know that Lord Perazim can make the asmodai take off their disguises and reveal themselves for what they really are," answered Garrett.

The troop began to pray in the secret language. Sekiah unfurled his red banner and waved it around the whole group. The flickers of light tried to escape, but they seemed trapped. As the flag whipped from side to side, the flashes of light began to dim until they became black. Sheriff Festus trembled with fear as he witnessed the metamorphosing of the glowing lights. Shrieking in agony, the asmodai finally revealed the hideousness of their true identity. The sheriff became enraged at the soldiers.

"How dare you torment our magickal friends!" he bellowed. "You have become enemies of this town! If Christiana's beseeching brought you here, then you have been summoned by the wrong power!"

Mounting up, Sekiah addressed the sheriff. "This town has been bamboozled!"

"No!" he retorted. "Just who do you think you are to condemn us and persecute our enchanted faeries? That 'fanatical woman'

Christiana, has brought these problems upon us - perchance she is a witch, after all!"

Giving a tug on the reins, their horses turned and the riders swiftly departed. As they came to a small bridge near the fallow field, it dawned upon Sir Tyler that their conversation with the sheriff might put Christiana in peril. They would have to go back!

Battle at Brookshire

Chapter 13

$\mathfrak{S}$ir Tyler and Garrett galloped down the dirt road along the fall planting field taking them around the backside of the village. They hoped their search for Christiana would not take long. Sir Spencer and Sekiah waited by the stone bridge that would lead them out of town.

Having returned to her humble cottage, Christiana neglected to close her door as she crossed the room and knelt by the corner chair to thank Prince Sabaoth for sending the knights. *"Perhaps the soldiers have come to convince the sheriff that Petronilla actually uses her powers and wisdom to put the town under her control,"* the maiden said to herself as hope breathed life into her fainting soul.

Christiana struggled to quiet her heart by calming her mind and focusing her attention on listening for the voice of Lord Perazim. As she waited for him to speak to her concerning her pleadings for Brookshire, the sound of pounding hoof beats drawing closer interrupted the maiden's solitude. Rising from her knees, she walked over to the doorway and saw one of the knights and his squire searching in earnest.

"Whom do you seek?" inquired the young woman.

"Maiden," Sir Tyler called out. "We have put you in great danger! Please come with us," the knight implored. "We are on our way to Brighton Castle and will take you there."

"But my place is here," Christiana said in protest.

"You stay at your own peril," answered the knight.

Pausing a moment, she submitted. Sir Tyler dismounted to lift her on the back of his horse and retreated once more across the bridge to meet up with Sir Spencer and Sekiah.

When he saw the soldiers departing the village, Sheriff Festus rushed over to the white witch's hovel. With great agitation, the sheriff burst through her open doorway. As he explained to the 'wise woman' what had transpired, Petronilla stopped the gentle push of her foot against the treadle, causing the soft rhythmic whirr of the spinning wheel to cease. Putting the wool fiber back in its basket, she arose from her stool with steel resolve in her bearing.

"Fetch the farmers from the spring planting field and gather the town's folk by the well," the witch ordered, without alarm.

The sheriff swiftly left to round up as many mortals in town as he could. He sent the blacksmith and the baker to bring the farmers in from the field. Shopkeepers quickly closed their businesses and tradesmen put down their work while Petronilla summoned the faeries and pixies. The time had come to reveal their strength and power.

Sir Spencer and Sekiah waited for the others. "Some mortals just want to remain bamboozled," said Sekiah in astonishment. Taking his sword and flailing it about in the air, Sekiah imagined himself doing spiritual warfare with his mortal weapons.

"We must be ready for a confrontation in case the others get caught while trying to rescue Christiana," the knight said to his squire.

As they focused their attention into the distance, the two observed the farmers coming into the town from the field. From their position they could not see the townspeople gathering by the well. Sitting in their saddles while keeping watch, Sir Spencer and Garrett called upon Prince Sabaoth to send his celestial army.

Sir Spencer turned his attention to the commotion in the center of the town where angry voices could be heard shouting. The other three had been surrounded by a mob of enraged villagers. Christiana, being pulled from Sir Tyler's horse, disappeared into the throng. Petronilla, standing away from the fray, believed that she directed the faeries and other-worldly creatures to various positions around the mortals. Invisible to the villagers, the asmodai swayed the mortals to riot the soldiers and 'the half-mad woman.'

"You must die!" yelled a farmer.

"Take the fanatical woman and burn her!" screamed the blacksmith. "She's evil!"

"Leave our faeries and pixies alone," cried another.

"Sir Spencer!" hollered Sekiah. "There's Christiana!"

She heard her name, looked up and saw the knight on the edge of the throng. Struggling to free herself from the grasp of the villagers, Christiana saw him deflecting away the attacks of the peasants as he made an opening to reach her. The maiden raised her arms as he swept her onto his horse and galloped away from the rabble.

Garrett and Sir Tyler, fending off the assaults on all sides, noticed the asmodai aiding the mortals. Suddenly, a terrifying sound caused the horses to rear. A strange elf-like creature rushed forth followed by a horde of other frightening spectres. The ghost-like apparitions were visible and horrifying. Having their spiritual armour on, fear could not penetrate Sir Tyler's and Garrett's raised shields. Quickly regaining control of their horses, knight and squire resisted the onslaught of the enemy. Just when it seemed that the soldiers had been overtaken by the inhabitants and the asmodai, they cried out to Prince Sabaoth in the secret language.

The battle shifted when the celestial army appeared. Riding out of the heavens, the huge warriors on massive steeds charged from every direction! The blazing white heavenly beings radiated the virtue, power and supremacy of King Elyon. The celestial warriors rushed the asmodai to take over the fight from the soldiers. The instant one of the hideous ghouls raised its sword to attack the mortals, a celestial warrior charged swiftly ahead to annihilate it. At this, the asmodai stopped in dismay.

The villagers, in a state of confusion, began to attack each other. Without the influence of the asmodai over them, the mortals became bewildered as to the purpose for their rage.

Taking their opportunity to flee, the soldiers swiftly joined together on the road to Brighton Castle.

Petronilla, upon witnessing the victory of the soldiers, gathered her garments about herself as she retreated to her hovel.

Sheriff Festus called out. "'Wise woman,' they were stronger than us. How can that be?"

"Only this time," she assured him. "The peasants need to become better trained in how to battle against spiritual soldiers. With that evil woman gone, it will be much easier to disciple the mortals."

The sheriff looked around in consternation at the village before him in utter chaos, "*How do I deal with this?!*" He asked aloud to himself.

Peaking out from behind the wreck and disarray the twinkle of pixie lights once again played in the open.

Brighton Castle

Chapter 14

𝔍atigued, the party travelled until the town fell from view. Finding a tranquil spot under the shade of a lofty alder, the riders dismounted. The horses wandered over to the tall grassy meadow where they contentedly grazed and drank from the refreshing creek nearby.

As the group settled themselves to rest under the tree, Christiana noticed blood trickling down Garrett's leg. In the heat of battle, the squire's wound had opened again.

"Lad," the maiden said. "You suffer injury."

"Let me take a look at your leg, Garrett," Sir Tyler said. "I have a little of the powder left that the widow gave me. You will also need another tourniquet. That pus makes me think it is once again infected."

Garrett winced. "Does it appear to be gangrene?" He grimaced.

"I cannot tell," answered Sir Tyler. "We must all ask King Elyon to heal your leg."

"Perhaps we should thank our Sovereign for already healing it," suggested Christiana."

"But it isn't healed," protested Garrett.

"Not in your body, yet," replied the maiden. "However, when we thank King Elyon in advance of our answer, we show Him great honour by our trust in Him. This moves His heart deeply toward us."

"I will try," said Garrett, feeling a little doubtful of Christiana's words.

When the attention to Garrett diminished, Sir Spencer introduced himself and his comrades to the maiden.

"Sirs," asked Christiana. "What errand brought you by way of Brookshire?"

"We were sent by our liege, Sir Roderick, to take an urgent message to King Waymon," answered Sir Tyler.

"We had been warned by Sir Leo about the town's rejection of King Elyon. However, we were quite taken aback by the sheriff's open display of contempt toward anyone who still chooses to believe in our invisible Sovereign. That hostility we found to be very bewildering."

"Ah, the sheriff…." Christiana sighed wistfully. "He and many more in Brookshire once served King Elyon with great devotion. When Petronilla fled her village and came to us, she offered to teach our children the traditions of her culture. She used her special way with the children to gain influence amongst the parents; and the parents did seek her guidance. Much of her counsel be wise, 'tis true, but it seemed to me that she wanted to take the place of Lord Perazim. For some of the parents, including Sheriff Festus, 'tis simpler to run to a mortal whom they see than to listen for instructions from the Immortal they cannot see."

With sadness in her voice, Christiana sighed again and then continued. "I have beseeched King Elyon much on behalf of my village. When I saw your flag and heard your discourse with Sheriff Festus, I was certain that King Elyon had sent you in answer to my cries. I find myself perplexed to be here with you on my way to Brighton Castle."

"Perhaps you will find your answer at the castle," replied Sekiah.

The afternoon still early and the prospect of reaching their destination after such an antagonistic confrontation brought an eagerness to the group to continue on their way. The throbbing pain in Garrett's leg quieted down and he too felt ready to travel on again. Sir Roderick had told them that it was a mere half day's journey from Brookshire.

"We shouldn't be long now in arriving at the castle," said Sir Spencer.

"As long as we don't fight anymore villains or meet any new dragons!" said Sekiah.

"I have no strength left in me to fight!" said Sir Tyler.

Garrett merely groaned at the idea.

The path led through a winding grove at the bottom of a great hill. Rounding the bend, the travelers finally made their way out of the stand of trees. The astonishing sight of Brighton Castle took their breath away. The gleaming white fortress loomed before them more majestically than anything imaginable! The great walled city went on for miles! Turrets festooned with cheerful pennants waved in the gentle breeze.

Sekiah made note to see if the castle flew all the flags of King Elyon. The rainbow, representing the covenant of King Elyon, fluttered above each turret with a separate emblem below that symbolized a different attribute of the Great King.

Red – Blood of Prince Sabaoth, Warfare and Fire
Gold – Kingship, Holiness, Liberty and Liberality
Silver – Redemption
Amber –The glory and Presence of King Elyon
Purple – Royalty, Honor, and Kingdom
Orange – Fire of King Elyon and also warfare
White – Purity, Innocence, Salvation, and
        Surrender to the Divine King
Blue – Grace, Mercy, Healing, the River of Life,

Green – Restoration and New Beginnings and
        Revelation

Sekiah noticed that the Black Pennant for the Gehenna of Judgment and Darkness was not flying. He thought to himself that it should be flying over Brookshire.

Crossing the open plain, the riders passed others also on their way to the castle. Many walking, a few like them on horseback and quite a number, obviously ill, lying on the hay in the back of horse–drawn wagons.

Garrett thought about the many stories of Brighton Castle that abounded far and wide of sick mortals coming and departing healed. King Waymon actually *helped* his poorer subjects who came to the castle in dire straits. He wanted his subjects to become prosperous!

Mortals, rich and poor, rulers and subjects alike, journeyed from far and wide to learn the secrets shared inside the walls of the great citadel.

The massive drawbridge remained lowered across the wide moat for the constant traffic of mortals and animals coming and going into the great stronghold from sunup to sundown.

"I know we have reached the celestial city!" laughed Garrett, as they crossed over the moat.

"I do not believe that the king of this fortress

would like to be confused with King Elyon!" retorted Sir Tyler.

"Can you imagine what the sovereign of this magnificent castle must be like?" Christiana wondered out loud.

"Regal," replied Garrett.

Arriving at the gate, Sir Spencer and Sir Tyler rode ahead of Christiana and the squires.

Dismounting, Sir Spencer inquired of the porter. "We have come to bring a message to the king from our liege, Sir Roderick of Bane Manor, and are in need of lodging overnight. The maiden with us is from the village of Brookshire and cannot go back."

"We have lodging accommodations for all you good folks, sir." The gate porter offered. "As for the lady, we will make sure that she has a place here, as well." The porter being sympathetic to Christiana's plight beckoned a page to bring a court attendant to care for her.

The group stood by a wall with the horses tethered to a post. Garrett sat on the ground leaning against the wall. The group found the sights and sounds in the courtyard quite entertaining while they waited on the page to return. They watched the busy mortals hustling and bustling about, small animals on the loose, children on the run and parents trying to take care of business. The clanging of the blacksmith's anvil and the tapping of a cobbler's hammer making shoes added to the already loud, cacophony of jarring sounds. Bane Manor had its own commotion, but nothing compared to the hubbub here!

Through the clamour of the courtyard the most melodious music came drifting down from an open window above. The sound of a choir practicing accompanied by minstrels playing their instruments so entranced them.

Looking over at Garrett, Christiana said with concern, "Garrett, your leg needs tending to. Your tourniquet soaks in blood yet again."

"Look over there where the infirmed are being taken," Sekiah said pointing across the way. "Perhaps there is a hospital here or a lady like the widow Robynne."

Finally, coming from the far side of the courtyard the page returned with a lady-in-waiting.

"Good afternoon, madam and sirs," addressed the page. "I am Dorian and this is Lady Suzanne." Noticing Garrett's bloody tourniquet, Dorian suggested the soldiers go first to the infirmary. The knights handed off their reins to Sekiah who walked the steeds over to a stable. Carefully they supported Garrett so he would not have to put any weight on his leg.

Lady Suzanne tenderly took Christiana by the arm and guided her through the courtyard.

"I feel very unlovely next to you," Christiana confided. "You are so beautiful and regal."

"You will not feel that way for very long, mum," the lady said comfortingly.

"I can't be any older than you, so please don't call me 'mum.'" Christiana implored.

"I have not been told your name," rejoined Lady Susanne.

"I suppose the introductions were not complete!" exclaimed the maiden. "My name is Christiana."

"Are you the one referred to as 'the devout lady of Brookshire?" asked the lady.

"Who knows of me here, my lady?" Christiana said taken aback.

"We have been pleading your cause to Great King Elyon for some time," Lady Suzanne replied. "The abbess at Beste Abbey came here by way of Brookshire and told us about you and how you have been carrying the burden for your village alone."

Upon hearing these words, Christiana began to tremble, and then fell into Lady Suzanne's arms sobbing.

"Why do you weep so, Christiana?" implored Suzanne.

"I imagined I carried my burden alone and it was so heavy to bear. My soul revives at this knowledge, Lady Suzanne." Christiana softly declared through her tears.

"We never carry our burdens alone!" exclaimed Lady Suzanne. "Prince Sabaoth always sends Lord Perazim to other mortals near or far to do warfare on behalf of those who are standing alone. It is one of the secret weapons that we wield! In your case, Prince Sabaoth sent to us Abbess Joan the Joyful."

The two young women walked together silently until they arrived at the keep where the inhabitants of the castle lived. Climbing the stairs, Lady Suzanne steadied Christiana up the unfamiliar rise of the irregular steps.

Opening a door, the lady ushered Christiana into the homey room. The maiden's attention went first to the open window on the far wall with a view upon the valley below. Bringing her focus back into the room, her gaze rested upon the furnishings that compared with her own simple household seemed quite handsome. The ample straw-filled bed with a cotton quilt positioned by the window looked most inviting. Next to the bed, on a sturdy nightstand under the window stood a tall white candle placed in a pewter holder. In the far corner sat a chair. On this side of the chair she noticed a stand with a wash basin and towels; on the adjacent wall, a small desk. Turning, Christiana saw on the other side of the doorway, a tall, darkly stained armoire for clothes and linens, which completed the room.

"Rest here while I arrange for a bath and change of clothes for you, dear Christiana."

The maiden walked over to the window and drew in a deep breath of fresh air that was more peaceful than any breath she had taken in many a year. Turning toward the lady, Christiana said marveling at the kindness of the lady-in-waiting. "You serve me as if I am her highness, the queen. I am but a mere peasant woman and not worthy of such consideration."

"Nonsense," dismissed Lady Suzanne. "I am the one honored to serve such a steadfast warrior of King Elyon!" Closing the door, the lady left to make arrangements for Christiana's care.

Looking out over the countryside, Christiana drank in the view from such a great height. In the far distance she spied her tiny village beyond the forest where she had come from earlier that same day. How long ago that journey seemed to her now! "My soul is being restored," Christiana uttered to herself through cleansing tears. Kneeling by the bed, the maiden thanked King Elyon for his tender mercies and for bringing her to this wonderful castle.

Weakened by the battle at Brookshire, Garrett tried not to pass out in the infirmary. The attendant treated the squire with great care as she soothingly applied a fresh poultice to the wound and gave him a tonic to drink to strengthen his fragile condition.

"I will escort you to your lodgings," Dorian stated.

"It will take too long for Garrett to hobble. We'd better link our arms together to carry young squire 'gimp.'" Sir Spencer said good-naturedly, linking arms with Sir Tyler.

As Dorian slowly led the soldiers across the inner courtyard to the keep, (the tower that housed guests of the castle as well as the place that stored many of the items needed in case of a siege. King Waymon and his court lived in the palace.) Sekiah related to the page about the recent adventures they had come through. Dorian exclaimed how he is looking forward to going on similar adventures when he becomes a squire.

Finding the steps to be rather tricky with the awkward position of carrying Garrett, Dorian directed them to separate rooms on a lower floor.

"I will see to it that each of you soldiers have bath water and a change of clothes," Dorian told them. "When you are ready, supper will be served in the grand hall. If you like, I will take you there when you have refreshed yourselves."

"Young page," Sir Tyler questioned. "Tell me what it's like to serve in such a splendid castle as this?"

"Unlike the pages that come from other castles to enter their service, I was born here. I know no other life," Dorian replied. "I would not choose another life, either."

"What is the king like?" inquired Sir Spencer.

"King Waymon loves all his subjects and knows that he is king under King Elyon. Someday he will have to present his stewardship of all the realm to Great King Elyon. I will bring your baths and changes of clothes now," Dorian said as he departed.

The comrades conversed with each other while Garrett rested in his room on his bed.

Being much refreshed but famished, the knights looked in on Garrett on their way to supper. Upon seeing him fast asleep, they let him remain undisturbed. Walking over to the great hall, Sekiah noticed two ladies walking ahead of them. Recognizing the Lady Suzanne, he realized that she must be walking with Christiana.

"Evening, ladies," greeted Dorian, who came to accompany the soldiers to the grand hall.

Turning around, Lady Suzanne responded, "Lovely evening, isn't it."

"Is that Christiana with you?" asked Sekiah.

"Yes, 'tis I," Christiana replied, beaming with delight. "I am dressed just like a princess!"

Both Sirs Spencer and Tyler could barely take their eyes off the lovely young woman before them. "You are not only dressed like a princess," Sir Tyler said in awe. "You have the bearing of one."

"We all look regal!" Sir Spencer exclaimed, as he laughingly took Lady Suzanne by the hand and gave her a sudden twirl.

Not to be outdone, Sir Tyler made a dramatically sweeping bow as he reached for Christiana's hand, saying, "my lady'," and waltzed her all the way to the steps of the grand hall.

Sekiah, turning to Dorian, who looked on in amusement asked, "May I have this dance?"

Snickering, Dorian answered, "Only if I can lead!"

The group enjoyed the pleasure of each other's company as they ate and shared stories about their lives and adventures. The soldiers sparred with each other using their humour and wit. Christiana could not recall a time she laughed with such unhindered enjoyment.

The long evening they would not soon forget.

Garrett's Dream

Chapter 15

&arrett slept peacefully, the tonic relaxing the squire giving him a restful night. Images floated in and out of his subconscious. Then in the wee small hours a dream settled into Garrett's mind.

From high above a large forest extending in all directions for miles, Garrett views the tops of the trees as the sun begins to set. On the far side of the forest a mountain range stretches across the horizon. In the foreground, Garrett takes note of a young peasant coming through the trees, hobbling on a single crutch. Garrett senses that this young mortal has journeyed from the other side of the mountains and has now come within reach of his destination. Before him lies a dirt road winding around a hill to a fortress. The unfaltering lad begins the steep ascent to the castle.

By the time he reaches the gatehouse, only the faint glow of twilight reveals the deserted courtyard. Crossing the grassy square, the traveler finds his way to a long, dark corridor. At the end and to the left, a bright light streams out into the hall from the doorway. Barely able to make it to the room, the peasant continues till he reaches the light.

Standing in the doorway, the youth leaning on his crutch is full of wonderment at the scene before him: Rows of long tables with peasants and serfs sitting across from each other eating and conversing. However, what amazes the lad most is the look of utter contentment upon each countenance.

At the front of the room the young mortal marvels at a table stretching nearly across the entire width. The table is filled with a bountiful array of delectable foods. Behind it stands a number of servers all dressed like royalty. As they enjoy each other's company, their attention is focused on the peasant before them whom they are serving. The servers dish up heaping helpings onto each plate.

To his astonishment, a peasant-woman rises from her place with dish in hand. "Could she possibly want more after the plateful she has already received?" *he wonders. With each step she takes to the serving table, the peasant-woman becomes transformed. The filth vanishes as her ragged and soiled clothes change into a beautiful new gown. On her head sits a tall conical hat with a sheer scarf draping down the back. Instead of filling her plate again, the royal lady steps behind the table to take her place in line to begin serving other peasants.*

Garrett awakes. What did this dream mean?

"Good morn, my faithful squire!" greeted Sir Tyler cheerily as he opened Garrett's door. "Fine squire Sir Roderick gave me!" teased the knight. "You are supposed to be taking care of me and yet here I am coddling you like a baby! And how are you this bright morn?"

Garrett, still coming out of his dream groaned under his covers trying not to lose the vision.

"Sir Tyler," Garrett said seriously, "I had a dream that seemed to have a message in it. Do you think someone could tell me what it means?"

"We are to have an audience with King Waymon today," replied Sir Spencer. "Perhaps he can tell you or direct us to someone who can. This place is miraculous and I am not surprised you had more than a restful night's sleep here. In the meantime, how is your leg doing?"

"I do not know yet," Garrett answered.

"I brought you a crutch," the knight said, producing the wooden aid. "It is unseemly for knights to carry their squire around!" Sir Spencer said in mock sarcasm.

Returning to the hallway, Sir Tyler watched as Christiana descended the steps. "Good morning, my fair lady," the knight happily declared.

"It certainly is," Christiana agreed.

"I am most ready for breakfast as soon as

my lolly-gagging squire gets himself out here!" Sir Tyler loudly announced good-naturedly.

Opening the door, Garrett presented himself, leaning on his new crutch. "Your ever-ready and most faithful squire presenteth himself!" he retorted.

It was slow going maneuvering the irregular steps. Garrett endured the bantering remarks of his companions all the way to the grand hall.

"How is Sir Spencer ever going to explain to the king that we are nursemaid to 'gimpy Garrett,' the hobbling squire?"

Being in rare form, Sir Tyler did not let the others off so easily, either. "We are quite the comrades to be introduced to the king!" the knight began. "First we have here our fearless leader, Sir Spencer." Rubbing his chin as if in serious contemplation, Sir Tyler intoned, "A knight who got himself seared by a fierce dragon. Hmm, 'Sir Smokey' would be suitable, or perhaps, 'Sir Spencer the Medium-Rare!'"

"You are very funny!" Sekiah laughed.

"Ah, young squire who serenades," Sir Tyler said. "I shall introduce you to his highness as 'Sekiah the warbling squire.'"

"And who shall you be introduced as?" asked Christiana.

"I?" Sir Tyler replied with comic grandiosity. "Why, I am 'Sir Tyler the Gallant' for having to endure my insufferable comrades!"

The retorts went flying between the friends all through breakfast, feeling very much like a continuation of the previous evening.

Dorian came to escort the group to the chamber of the king. Approaching the reception room, their demeanor became subdued.

"I wonder what his majesty is like," Garrett said quietly.

Coming to the massive doors of the chamber, they noticed the sentry stationed at attention as they supposed there would be for a king. The sentry opened the door on the right for the guests to enter. Although not an overly large or ornate room as the massive doors would suggest, the rich wood paneling and exquisite decorative touches made the area attractive and inviting. Several large vases held in them an abundance of freshly cut spring flowers filling the room with bright bouquets of variegated colors and overwhelming floral fragrance. The late morning sun streaming through the open windows cheered the otherwise dark chamber.

Once ushered in, they stood before a very tall mortal with short graying hair and steel blue eyes that looked into one's soul with transparent directness. His worn face and powerful hands displayed the scars from past battles. In spite of the king's imposing bearing, he possessed a disarming meekness.

King Waymon addressed Dorian, "Would you care to introduce these fine visitors to me."

"Yes, Grandpa," Dorian replied.

"No wonder he wouldn't want to have any other kind of life!" thought Garrett.

After Dorian made the formal presentations he slipped out. Inviting his visitors to make themselves comfortable in the chairs and couches, the king asked each one about himself and made light of Garrett's injury for he had received many battle wounds of his own. They quickly learned that King Waymon loved to joke and enjoyed a good laugh. Feeling at ease, the group soon told him of the mock introductions they had teased each other about. The king told stories on Sir Roderick that the young soldiers knew for certain their liege would never tell on himself!

"Young maiden," the king said, turning his attention to Christiana. "Your burdens are not unknown to us here at the palace. However, King Elyon has not called upon us to intervene in matters concerning Brookshire, except through spiritual warfare. Our great Sovereign sets circumstances right and brings justice in ways that are mysterious to mortals; even to kings and nobles."

"Now," began the king, looking at Sir Spencer, "You have come with a message for me from Sir Roderick."

"Yes," replied Sir Spencer in all seriousness. "Your heralds, Cedric and Cole were waylaid by Vikings in our lord's forest."

"Apparently they are alive, since you know their names," said the sovereign.

"Cedric was found unconscious and left for dead. Cole has been taken captive."

Allowing the gravity of the news to settle upon him, the king lowered his head and folded his hands together, his index fingers gently tapping against his pursed lips.

"I am aware of Viking settlements among us, but I have not heard news of any recent attacks until now," King Waymon said. "How is Cedric?" he asked.

"Your herald recovers, Your Majesty," answered Sir Spencer.

"This casts a shadow upon the tournaments," the king said, gazing out the window. "I must consult with my advisers concerning this matter."

"There is more to be discussed," the sovereign stated. "We shall resume our conversation later this afternoon."

"Yes, Your Highness," Sir Spencer answered.

"Dorian shall come for you when I am ready," King Waymon said.

The group departed the chambers and passed the hours of the afternoon uneventfully.

Dorian came running across the courtyard to where the soldiers and the maiden sat together commenting to each other of the interesting observations each made as they watched the mortals going about their business.

"The king awaits your return, maiden and sirs," beckoned Dorian. The group rose and followed the page once more to the king's chambers.

The opportunity eventually came for Garrett to ask the king about his dream.

"Instead of explaining your dream to you, I will show you a demonstration of it," answered King Waymon. "Let me know when you think you understand the things you observe."

The group left the chamber and made their way into the commotion of the large courtyard. King Waymon explained the various activities and described some of the mortals they watched.

"Do you see that blind woman?" he pointed to. "She works in the dispensary."

"She's blind!" exclaimed Sekiah.

"Yes, but 'Blind Jessie' has an extra-ordinary ability King Elyon has blessed her with," explained the king. "She witnessed many horrors in her young life when her village was raided and burned by Vikings. Her entire family perished and she saw them die. The trauma caused her to lose her eyesight."

"How long has she been here?" asked Garrett.

"She was brought here about seven years ago by Sir Leo the Dragonslayer," answered King Waymon. "Sir Leo and his knights arrived too late to save the village, but they did manage to rescue Jessie and two other peasants. Her progress was slow to begin with," the king continued. "At first she wanted to die, however, with the gentle care of the women in the castle her will to even live was restored. Now she won't take guff from anybody!" King Waymon chuckled.

"Over there," the king continued, "that is my high constable, Sir Graham. He is now commander-in-chief of the garrison. In a strategic battle, he neglected to use his shield of Faith and he fell captive to the asmodai. After being enslaved to them for quite awhile, he finally realized how he lost. When the knight cried out to Prince Sabaoth to help him find his shield, the Prince sent the celestial warriors to help him fight his way to freedom. Now Sir Graham is one of my most mighty worship warriors. His new shield is even stronger than the first one and he keeps it with him at all times."

"The boy that Sir Graham is conversing with helps the marshal who is in charge of all the stables. He is very good with animals and the animals are good for the lad. He was abused as a young child and blamed for many things he did not do. The lad experiences kindness here as well as learning how to stand up for himself.

"Everyone has a story to tell," King Waymon went on. "Some are broken in spirit, some are broken in body and some are broken in their souls. Mortals come here from abroad because they have heard the many stories of how others have been healed and restored. Some stay while others return."

Looking at Garrett, the king noted that the lad began to understand the meaning of his dream.

"How do all these mortals get healed?" asked Garrett.

"Some receive a miracle, which is an instant healing and others are healed through the process of time. That means they often have their physical wounds attended to by a doctor or practitioner in medicinal herbs.

"If the wound is in the heart or mind, we have teachers and counselors who instruct them in how to apply the healing balm of the Holy

Scroll. Most of the instructors were once in need of healing themselves. They understand the pain many mortals suffer and can administer Truth in love. Sometimes Truth is gentle and soothing. Other times, Truth is direct and if not received, will cause offense. Some of those mortals left and have even tried to stop others from coming."

"Christiana," King Waymon said, abruptly changing the subject. "I have already spoken to Lady Elizabeth. She is over the worship leaders who perform our dancing and expressive signing. Lady Elizabeth would be delighted to have you come to her classes. She will teach you new ways to intercede as well as giving strength to your own spirit for the battle you are waging on behalf of your village. King Elyon has unfinished business in Brookshire. While you are here, you will hear from him concerning his plans."

A tear slipped down Christiana's cheek unnoticed by herself but not by King Waymon. She was a tender plant in need of fresh soil and care.

"Dorian told me that you plan on leaving today," King Waymon said to the others. "It is already time for supper and I would implore you to stay through tomorrow. I will give you the message for Lord Roderick at that time. Tomorrow, you will experience Celebration Day at Brighton Castle. It is always the highlight of our week and we never know exactly what to expect. When Lord Perazim chooses, he directs the celebration. We never know when he will choose to, and we must always be prepared to follow his will. We are never disappointed," the king finished with a smile and delight in his eyes.

What could they say? Of course the group was thrilled to be asked to stay for such a festive day. They could hardly wait!

Celebration Day

Chapter 16

Rain drizzled softly on the open ledge collecting into a pool of water spilling over the edge, dribbling down the wall and splattering into a puddle on the floor. A small puff of cool damp air gently wafted into the room. Through the drowsy haze of sleep Garrett slowly became conscious of the throbbing pain in his leg. Trying to resist fully waking, he worked unsuccessfully to get comfortable again. *"How long before it finally heals?"* he wondered irritably. *"Some 'day of celebration' with this rain!"* Garrett grumbled to himself. *"This would be a perfect day to spend in bed."* Being in no mood to celebrate anything, he tried once more to snuggle under the warmth of the cozy comforter.

The blaring trumpet announcing the start of a new day jolted the squire out of his disgruntled reverie. Hunger gave Garrett reason enough to get up and dress. Groaning as each movement exacerbated the burning pain of his wound, the young soldier gingerly rose and stumbled to the basin. Splashing cold water in his face to wash the sleep from his eyes sent chills across Garrett's body causing him to shiver. This triggered a streak of pain to run down the lad's leg. Gasping from the coldness of the water and the shock of pain in his leg, Garrett lunged for his tunic. Exhausted and out of breath from his early morning ordeal, the squire finally finished dressing and emerged from his room famished and ready for breakfast.

Opening the door to the stairway, Garrett could hear the cheerful voices of his friends as they excitedly greeted one another. Garrett hoped that by closing his door, the others would pass on by, though he knew he could not escape so easily. Trapped! And he could not hide his foul mood, either.

"Good morn, Garrett!" chirped Christiana. "Is this not a day full of great expectation!"

"With this rain?" was all Garrett could mutter.

"Oh," said Sekiah, "You are not your usual merry self. What's wrong?"

"My leg hurts," complained Garrett, "and it's raining. What kind of celebration can we have on a day like this?"

"It's only sprinkling a little," answered Sir Tyler. "And besides, we'll be inside, anyway."

"Come on, Garrett," coaxed Sekiah. "Rain or shine, pain or no pain, this is going to be a great day!"

"Why don't you all go ahead and I'll hobble on over after you." Garrett suggested. "I don't want to dampen–get it–'dampen' your spirits."

"You know," spoke up Sir Spencer, "some days I wake up grumpy and some days I just let him sleep in," he joked.

"That's pretty funny!" laughed Sekiah.

"You know, Garrett," Christiana said seriously. "You have authority over your emotions. You can either choose to change your mood or you can ask us to help you if you feel overwhelmed by it. King Elyon has something very significant for all of us today and you will be in danger of missing out if you continue giving into this irritability."

"Yes, Christiana," Garrett conceded. "Perhaps when we get inside the cathedral my mood will change."

"Yes," chimed in Sir Spencer. "As slow as you go, he will have lots of time to change that grouchy mood you are in."

"Always the well-spoken knight!" Sir Tyler chided.

"Ok, enough attention on me," Garrett said impatiently. "Let's go to breakfast."

Slogging through the puddles and the slowly falling raindrops, the little group found the grand hall nearly deserted by the time they arrived. They ate quickly.

Stepping back through the doorway to the open courtyard, each one gasped. The radiant sun and blue sky had broken through the dispersing clouds displaying an unexpected rainbow shining in brilliant colors right above the castle.

Noting the sun breaking through the overcast, Dorian remarked, "The rain has stopped and the sun is shining."

"King Elyon still keeps his solemn pledge to us," Christiana stated.

"That rainbow looks so beautiful above the rainbow pennants on the turrets," commented Sekiah. The others agreed.

Trudging through the soggy grass and around mud puddles, the party neared the cathedral. The powerful music resounded from across the courtyard.

"Locke Cathedral is almost as large as Beste Abbey!" Sekiah commented as they marveled at its' grandeur.

As the group kept a slow pace for Garrett's sake, others hurried by to get in before the service began. Approaching the entrance, the carved doors painted a bright red stood like sentries on either side of the doorway. On the wall inside the narthex, Sekiah read the words under a stained glass depiction of Prince Sabaoth triumphantly standing over Asmo: *"He holds the keys to Death and Hades."* The exuberant sounds from inside the sanctuary of the cathedral drew their attention away from admiring anymore beautiful windows.

Just inside, Dorian watched for the group. "The king has asked me to escort you to the front where your places are reserved," he said, turning to lead the visitors. "Christiana," Dorian added, "Lady Suzanne has asked for you to sit with her." Pleased, Christiana walked down the aisle looking ahead for her new friend.

Then, the horns trumpeted from the balcony on either side of the platform drawing the attention of all to the front. Tambourines banged and jangled in rhythm of the pounding drums. The hurdy-gurdy and bagpipes joined in along with the recorder and harpsichord. The cacophony of jubilant sounds overwhelmed the newcomers.

"This reminds me of a festival." Garrett said to Sekiah.

Both the adults and the youth formed a line in stately procession from opposite directions in front of the steps to the chancel. Some carried flags while others began to move in flowing, leaping gestures. The choir loft behind the chancel was filled with choristers of all ages.

Loudly singing and clapping their hands they joyfully led the congregation in songs of celebration. The immense interior of the cathedral became engulfed by the display of sound and visual presentation inviting the presence of King Elyon to come among his subjects.

Garrett's senses felt overwhelmed by the spectacle. Leaning on his crutch, he stood with the rest of the assembly. From the corner of his eye Garrett saw that King Waymon could not even stay by his seat – caught up in the spirit of the music and dance, the king could not help but clap his hands and even do his own little jig! Turning to look around, Garrett watched many others in the aisles also dancing.

"Oh, how I long to dance like those around me!" he said out loud.

After several songs, Bishop Bryan walked up to the front of the pulpit. "We welcome all those here for the first time," he said, addressing the visitors. The congregation clapped enthuse-iastically and greeted those around them.

"What a boisterous place this is!" Sir Tyler said, leaning over to Sir Spencer.

"'Tis a grand spectacle," Sir Spencer replied. "I wish Devynne were here, for she would take great delight in such a display!"

"Christiana seems to be taking it all in. I am glad that Queen Raewynne has Lady Suzanne keeping her company," Sir Tyler commented.

"Truly the maiden has need of gentle care and a kind friend," Sir Spencer added.

"It is time now for the tithes and offering part of our celebration," the bishop continued. "We show our gratefulness for the provision King Elyon has blessed us with by returning to him a tenth of the increase on the bounty we have gathered. Whether from our crops or from our business, it is King Elyon who gives us the ability to take care of our needs."

Cheers and wild clapping rose from the congregation. The minstrels and choristers rejoiced with music as the baskets passed throughout the rows.

"Everyone behaves as if this were a gala affair!" commented Sekiah.

"Exactly," answered Dorian. "It is all about demonstrating our affection to King Elyon and Prince Sabaoth."

The energetic songs of adoration gradually changed to reverence. The drums quieted and the flutes and viols replaced the trumpets. The lute and psaltery were accompanied by the pipe, the tabor and the harp. The dancers, in long sweeping movements brought the congregation to focus on the presence of King Elyon. Lady Elizabeth swirled gracefully in slow motion, her white and gold flags softly flowing. Then she bowed on her knees with her arms stretched in front of her on the ground. The atmosphere became still. A sense of anticipation fell upon the assembly as the congregation waited in complete silence. After a long pause, the queen arose.

In a crowd of varying degrees of poverty and wealth, her stately grandeur commanded the attention of all. Walking up the steps to the center of the chancel, Queen Raewynne stood in front of the altar. Her majesty's sumptuous long gown ornamented by heavy gold cording and embellished with intricate lace highlighted the stunning purple dress. The queen's final adornment, her bejeweled tiara, sparkled as it sat upon her long dark tresses.

Queen Raewynne scanned the faces looking up at her in anticipation. With joy in her heart, the queen began. "King Elyon has a word for us this morn. He is pleased with your celebration of his beloved son, Prince Sabaoth. Lord Perazim has come to move among us and to heal anyone in need." Breaking forth into the secret language, Queen Raewynne danced in place.

"*Hallelujah!*" she shouted. "Some of you have come here for the first time and marvel at what you have witnessed. We celebrate our celestial Prince who rescued us from the Gehenna of Judgment. The perfect blood that poured out of

Prince Sabaoth's body when he died was the currency paid to save our mortal souls. This same blood also cures our diseases and removes all curses put on us from the Great Fall. Prince Sabaoth's death was mortal but his power is immortal. That is why we receive everything through faith – faith, which is believing in what he did for us, brings the immortal into the mortal realm. Come now to receive your healing and salvation!" the queen said earnestly.

Ministers, grown-ups and youth, stood at the front of the altar to call upon King Elyon for those in need. Others stood behind the ones in need to catch them as they fell under the power of Lord Perazim. Dorian and Lady Suzanne left their seats to minister. A knight having returned from the Crusades passed around the holy oil from Jerusalem to anoint the sick.

Sekiah recognized many of the mortals coming down the aisle as those he had seen crossing the plain when they first arrived at the castle.

Garrett could not move quickly enough to avoid the near crushing from the onslaught of those coming to the front. Finally able to make his way forward, he limped toward a short stocky fellow with thick, calloused hands.

"What have you need of young squire?" the minister inquired.

"I sustained a wound in battle and the injury does not heal," Garrett answered.

Laying a surprisingly gentle hand on Garrett's forehead, the minister lifted his voice, "King Elyon, this faithful squire has been wounded in battle. We ask in your name and with the authority that comes with it, heal this soldier's leg!"

A sudden weakness came upon Garrett causing him to fall backward. Strong arms supported him as he descended to the floor. Lying there, he had a vague awareness of others coming down on either side of him. Some cried softly, others laughed. A warm peace hovered over Garrett while he rested. Heat radiated from his wound. Others having gone forward now returned to their benches healed. Garrett remained on the floor.

The musicians continued playing as the healings continued. The scene was unlike any the group had ever witnessed before.

"Why do all these mortals fall on the ground?" Sekiah wondered aloud.

"Because Lord Perazim's presence over-powers them," replied Dorian, who had returned to his seat next to Sekiah.

"I can already tell that we have had an exciting visitation from Lord Perazim this morning!"

Bishop Bryan exclaimed. "Any visitation is exciting!"

"Hallelujah!" shouted someone in the middle of the congregation.

Garrett eventually sat up, awkwardly trying to scoot himself back to his place on the bench, Sekiah and Dorian bent down to lift him up. But it finally took Sirs Spencer and Tyler to hoist the limp squire to his seat.

"My leg is healed!" Garrett exclaimed. "The pain is gone! I can walk without the crutch."

His companions rejoiced with him. Garrett danced in front of the chancel a high-spirited dance, twirling and spinning and jumping as he clapped his hands and pounded his feet.

"Lord Perazim has come and moved among us this morning," the bishop stated enthusiastically. "May peace and tranquility refresh you this afternoon for the service tonight." With that, Bishop Bryan retreated through the side door of the chancel to take off his vestments, or clerical robes, in the sacristy.

King Waymon and Queen Raewynne rose first to walk down the center aisle of the nave to the narthex followed by the king's page and queen's lady-in-waiting. Pausing by the pew where the young knights and their squires sat, King Waymon extended an invitation to the soldiers. "Please dine at my table," the king said.

"Thank you, Sire," all replied in unison.

"Dinner will be filled with jocularity at the king's table!" Sekiah said excitedly. The others agreed.

Arriving at the long table in the courtyard abundantly spread with all manner of savory dishes, the king beckoned the group to sit at his end.

"It is too lovely of a day to eat in the grand hall," remarked the queen.

"It is indeed, Ma'am," replied Sir Tyler.

"Garrett," addressed Christiana. "I see that you went forward to appeal to King Elyon to heal you. You are walking without your crutch. I am pleased that your mood this morning did not prevent you from receiving the gift of healing from Lord Perazim."

"I think it was Lord Perazim's over-whelming presence that changed me." Garrett confessed.

Bishop Bryan met the group as he approached the table. The members of the party introduced themselves to him.

"I grew up with Lord Roderick and Lady Isabelle," the bishop said.

The balmy afternoon resounded with the laughter of everyone sitting in the company of the king. The queen and bishop joined in to entertain the guests with stories of Sir Roderick and Lady

Isabelle, as well as relating their own tales of misadventures.

The youth had started a game on the far side of the courtyard. Dorian invited Garrett and Sekiah to join in. The three raced each other over to where the sport had just begun. Garrett played hard. The return of his strength felt wonderful!

As the afternoon sun slowly slipped across the sky, the deepening shadows leisurely stretched across the courtyard. A trumpet sounded the call that the service would soon begin. Garrett, Sekiah and Dorian ran past the king's table on their way to the cathedral. The king's party stood to their feet and joined the others returning. "

"What will Lord Perazim do this evening?" Sir Spencer asked as they entered the vestibule.

"Whatever it is," replied Queen Raewynne, "It is never what you might expect."

Supernatural Weapons

Chapter 17

A sense of anticipation hung in the air as each mortal entered the grand and beautiful cathedral. The little group walked down the aisle once more to the triumphant music already resounding throughout the majestic church.

As the members of the group took their seats, each wondered. *"How can we receive anymore after all we have experienced this morning?"*

Dorian watched the squire's reaction to things that were normal for him but new to them. He liked the soldiers that had come to Brighton Castle and hated to see them depart.

Bishop Bryan walked up the stairs to the chancel and took his place behind the podium. "Here we are again," he began. "It is hard to realize how fast this afternoon went! But I am ready for the surprises that Lord Perazim has in store for us this evening, are you?"

The entire congregation exploded into a wild uproar of cheering and loud clapping. Everyone stood to their feet and some even ran down the aisles with a burst of excitement that they could not contain.

Garrett caught himself jumping up and down and shouting right along with the rest of the congregation. No one felt inhibited in an atmosphere of such freedom. The desire for King Elyon's presence even caused Bishop Bryan to dance a little dance.

Sitting on his throne, King Elyon laughed with delight at the joyful invitation ascending from Brighton Castle invoking his presence. He gladly accepted the request!

"Lord Perazim," The bishop began, "Give me your words to speak and give your mortals ears to hear. Amen.

"As mortal combatants in spiritual warfare, we must learn about the supernatural weapons that King Elyon has supplied. We must also learn the difference between our bona fide power and the bogus power of Asmo. Asmo cannot create anything with his power; he can only imitate and twist, or pervert what Prince Sabaoth does. He uses his bogus power to lure mortals to their ultimate destruction." The bishop paused as he looked upon the intent expressions on the faces of his congregation.

Christiana felt a stab of pain in her heart as she thought of her little village of Brookshire. How she had wept for her deceived neighbors. *"Nearly everyone there worships Asmo,"* she thought to herself, *"yet they argue that they don't."*

Bishop Bryan continued. "As long as this world is under siege, mortals live in enemy territory until Prince Sabaoth finally sends Asmo and his minions to the Gehenna of Judgment once and for all.

"Asmo has power that is stronger than any mortal's ability to resist because he is not mortal, he is an immortal spirit. Only when a mortal uses the supernatural weapons supplied by King Elyon can he win against the unseen enemy.

"The Lord High Chancellor, Lord Perazim, comes from King Elyon's throne room in the celestial city to move throughout the entire world on his behalf to help us in our battles. He trains, comforts, and convicts to develop discipline in us to carry out our assignments.

Elaborating, the bishop explained, "Mortal soldiers sustain wounds, become discouraged, lose direction, do not always recognize the enemy and need help from each other and King Elyon. So, there are nine specific weapons that Lord Perazim makes available to each mortal as he determines. This way, we all work together to help each other.

"After we learn what these weapons are, we will ask Lord Perazim to bestow upon us the weapons of his choosing. Then we will need to conduct training exercises to acquire the skills in the use of these supernatural weapons.

"I will begin with Wise Counsel," said the bishop. "The definition of wise counsel is giving the best advice based on the information available. But Lord Perazim offers supernatural direction that gives the correct solution."

"I certainly did not ask Lord Perazim for wise counsel or listen to my comrades when I was enticed by that Keltoi chieftain," Sir Spencer grimaced at the recollection. *"Because I listened to the wrong voice I ended up captive down in the Caverns of Cataclysmic Calamities! This is one supernatural gift I am certainly going to ask Lord Perazim for!"*

"Clear Understanding," the bishop went on. "Lord Perazim reveals knowledge to a mortal concerning a current situation and insight on how to resolve an issue. That mortal speaking to you does not know what just happened to you or your request to King Elyon."

"Next, we will talk about Trust," Bishop Bryan stated. "There are different levels and types of trust, which we often call faith. There is faith to believe in our invisible Sovereign; faith to believe for other's needs and for supernatural provision and healing. The only way we can use our spiritual weapons is by faith.

The bishop continued. "Asmo does not want your health, your wealth, or anything that belongs to you. He only wants your faith because he knows that if you lose your faith in King Elyon he has *YOU*. If he can make you doubt the existence of King Elyon or his power, then he has won.

"It is imperative to always - at all times - keep your shield of faith raised against the fiery darts of the enemy. You are under constant attack. Asmo does not rest. He does not relent. Your entire life as a warrior and future ruler with King Elyon depends upon whether you have maintained your shield of faith. The many great acts that we perform are not done to earn our place in immortality but to demonstrate our love and faith in our Sovereign.

Bishop Bryan went onto the next supernatural weapon. "Healing is for the purpose of restoring any part of our body, mind or emotions that is not performing according to the way the Holy Scroll says it should. King Elyon does not want us to be sick. He wants us to have a full and satisfying life right here on earth!"

Sekiah saw his friend out of the corner of his eye looking down at his leg. Gratitude trickled down Garrett's face in the form of a tear.

"Who in this meeting received a healing in your body this morning?" Bishop Bryan asked. Hands raised, some leapt to their feet and others yelled out. "Many in here had the faith to believe that King Elyon wants them healed!

"Miraculous Powers," said the bishop, "are demonstrations of the supernatural abilities of King Elyon. Some examples of this are creative miracles such as withered limbs growing, the dead raised to life....Did anyone receive that miracle this morning?" asked the bishop.

Garrett bolted from the pew. "I am a squire from Bane Manor," he began. "My comrades and I encountered the Keltoi on our way here. During their attack on us, I let my shield down and was hit in the leg by an arrow. It was my own fault!" Garrett said with regret in his voice. "I am a war dancer and thought I might not ever dance again. But this morning, a minister called out to King Elyon for me and my leg was instantly healed!" he shouted.

"Praise to King Elyon!" shouted many in the congregation, along with thunderous applause as Garrett danced a jig and then went into an all-out war dance, twirling and spinning and jumping. The minstrels picked up his rhythm and joined in with a spontaneous melody.

"I believe that we have witnessed a great example of a healing miracle," Bishop Bryan joyfully proclaimed.

"Although I am not doing the comparison this evening between the bogus power of Asmo and real power of King Elyon with each supernatural ability," said the bishop. "I feel it is important to do so regarding this particular supernatural power. Mortals are so intrigued by the phony razzle-dazzle of Asmo's super powers. His use of witchcraft including levitation, enchantments, which is the same as casting spells, fortunetelling and other forms divert you away from King Elyon."

The four comrades remembered their encounter with the Keltois.

Sekiah whispered to Garrett, "Remember that girl the sorcerer levitated?"

"Yes," replied Garrett, "He was good at using trickery."

"....Even healing the sick or raising the dead," Bishop Bryan continued. "If Asmo can put a disease on you, he can take it off!" exclaimed the bishop. "It sometimes looks identical to the real, so you must stay in close communication with Lord Perazim to discern the difference when it is not obvious.

"Next is Prophecy," said the bishop. This supernatural ability is used by King Elyon to speak his words through a mortal to give insight into a future situation, or to infuse courage and confidence into someone. We usually say to 'encourage.'"

Queen Raewynne could not sit still any longer. Jumping up and shouting "Praise to King Elyon!" she walked over to Christiana and bent down face to face with her. "Isn't it awesome to have a ruler who can direct our lives from the end of it? You may have terrible decisions to make in your future but Lord Perazim can give you knowledge and understanding to know what decision you should make. Some decisions won't look like they will bring about a happy ending, but all our happy endings don't take place here on earth! 'Happily ever after' sometimes happens when we enter King Elyon's realm!" Just as abruptly as she got up to prophecy, the queen sat back down.

Stunned by the sudden message from the queen, Christiana pondered her words and wondered at the courage she felt beginning to flow into her being.

"Thank you, your majesty," the bishop said to the queen. Addressing the congregation he pointed out, "That is an excellent demonstration of the gift of prophecy.

"Moving onto the next supernatural skill we will explain what is meant by Distinguishing between Spirits. There are four types of spirits that we must distinguish between: King Elyon, celestial warriors, Asmo, along with the asmodai, and mortals. It is vitally important to know just who and what we are dealing with. Too often the wrong action is taken because we do not recognize the voice we are listening to or the hidden motive behind a deed."

"We come to the ninth super gift," Bishop Bryan declared. "The Secret Language is what we use to keep our spirit connected with King Elyon, who is the King of all spirits. This helps mortals to get out of the realm of earth and our five senses and into the realm of faith. Faith is of the spirit – and the spirit realm is where our victories are won.

"Asmo can no longer enter into the throne room of heaven where military strategies are planned," affirmed the bishop. "When we speak in the secret language, our words cannot be intercepted by the asmodai, but they penetrate straight through enemy lines to the war counsel in heaven. This is also one of our spiritual weapons. We pray this way for Lord Perazim to give us strength and to foil the plots of our enemy. We are able to make proclamations and state our requests perfectly in the secret language. Lord Perazim is actually speaking through us – all battles are won or lost by words. The universe and our world were created by words. So Lord Perazim uses us to speak the words that will bring our victory.

"It was words that freed me from the asmodai," Garrett thought back to the forest, *"I knew I had to sing out loud with words in order to move."*

Bishop Bryan continued. "Some mortals speak to a group in the secret language and then Lord Perazim gives the translation to someone else. It is another means that King Elyon likes to use to include mortals in the plans of his throne room.

Then the bishop walked around the pulpit and step down to the floor. "When was the last time *you* influenced King Elyon's Royal Counsel?" he asked looking into several faces. "We have that kind of power, you know. Prince Sabaoth gave it to us. *What* do you talk to King Elyon about? *Who* do you talk to our Great Sovereign on behalf of?" Bishop Bryan paced back and forth. "Me and mine or the things that are on King Elyon's heart? If you become one of the strategists in King Elyon's war room, the king will make certain that you and your needs shall not be forgotten."

Bishop Bryan called for the ministers to stand if front of the steps to the chancel and lay hands on all those asking Lord Perazim to give them the supernatural weapons.

The ministers also asked that these mortals would develop the character of Lord Perazim to help them not become proud with their new powers.

The fellow soldiers moved quickly to the front. Before the minister even touched Garrett, he began to jump and shout. Joy overwhelmed him. Garrett already spoke in the secret language, but he started to sing like he had never sung before. Garrett nearly knocked Sekiah to the ground in his exuberance.

"Fire is shut up in your bones!" the minister shouted to Garrett as he touched him with the palm of his hand on his forehead. "In the name of Lord Perazim this fire will consume you and you will receive more supernatural powers and weapons for your arsenal. You and your comrade will be sent forth together to do many great exploits in the name of Prince Sabaoth."

Garrett felt himself shake as intense heat and light gushed from his bones throughout his entire body. *"How amazing,"* thought Garrett, *"that something spiritual can be felt in my physical body!"*

Sir Spencer and Sir Tyler fell down laughing uncontrollably. "I must be drunk!" Sir Spencer gasped.

"I have never felt this way before!" Sir Tyler said between hysterics. "I am partial to this strange manifestation!"

Christiana wept in Suzanne's arms as the Spirit moved in her being. She felt an unwavering focus taking place to be obedient to whatever King Elyon asked of her.

Many mortals lingered basking awhile longer in the heavy cloud of Lord Perazim's presence as it slowly lifted.

Coming out of the cathedral, the foursome staggered together as they worked to support each other back to their rooms.

"We must needs be sober by the morn for the recommencement of our journey." Sir Tyler said, trying to sound authoritative.

"For the *what*?" snorted Garrett.

"Resuming of our journey," stated Sir Spencer as he shoved Garrett in light-hearted fun.

"This perchance may well be the most wonderful sensation!" announced Sekiah.

"Pray let me never to be sober again!" Sir Spencer declared.

"Is this the laughter that Abbess Joan the Joyful talked about that King Elyon put in her soul?" asked Garrett.

"I imagine that it is!" answered Sir Tyler. "Henceforth from this day foreword I decree," intoned Sir Tyler, "that Abbess Joan the Joyful shall be forever known as 'Jolly Joan.'"

Walking unsteadily through the dark courtyard in the crisp night air, each one looked up into the black sky sparkling with brilliant stars. Staring into the vast depths of the universe intensified each one's awareness of their finite mortality.

"King Elyon is beyond comprehension to have created all this and beyond," Garrett said in awe.

"He certainly is a wonder to behold," affirmed Sir Tyler.

Setting the Stage for War:

Asmo's Plot

Chapter 18

$\mathbf{A}$smo seethed with loathing. The obnoxious sounds of joy and celebration that resonated forth from Brighton Castle not only echoed throughout the atmosphere, they rose as if on celestial wings straight through the universe of time and space and into eternity!

Brighton Castle, King Elyon's crowning jewel on his pet planet. Asmo hated Brighton Castle and all that it stood for. From this fortress mortals learned to love their invisible Sovereign. From this citadel worship warriors made up of dancers, singers, minstrels and armour bearers marched forth into the rest of the tiny planet to teach other mortals about their invisible Creator. They also learned how to fight against their arch enemy Asmo. This went on year after year and each successive turn of the calendar only emboldened the king to broaden his sphere of influence.

"I have endured ENOUGH!" bellowed Asmo. His eyes like slits glowed as burning orange and black embers. "I must devise a plan to once and for all destroy this stronghold. But how shall I attack?" Asmo pondered aloud as he hovered high above the magnificent edifice.

"Hmmmmm." Gently stroking his short stubbly beard, the emperor of Valois studied the map open before him. The map lay across the large ornately carved table in his lavish chambers. A warm fire crackled in the impressive fireplace across the room, warming the atmosphere with its heat and light. But the emperor did not notice. The days now growing longer and warmer ushered in a restless wander lust causing the emperor to only have thoughts of adventure and conquest. Court life bored him with its myriad aspects of intrigue and drama. The tedious duties and obligations that demanded his attention wearied the emperor.

"What better way to flee zee confines of so great a fortress zan to seek out an invasion," the monarch said to himself. "King Waymon grows old and has become complacent een recent years. He forgets zee grudge I hold against him. Britanniae eez ripe for zee picking," the monarch said to himself. "Eet eez yet spring and we have plenty of time for a long siege that weell weaken zeir weell to resist. Zeze time I shall not be denied satisfaction. My domain shall encompass all of Britanniae and eets inhabitants weell become my subjects," the emperor said gloating at the prospect of advancing his kingdom.

Asmo flew above the palace and over to the cathedral where sinister looking gargoyles decorated the flying buttresses of the religious building. Straddling the jutting downspout of the stone monster, Asmo stroked the grotesque head as he scornfully laughed to himself. "Mortals are so easy to manipulate!" he sneered, then added, "While the *great emperor* gathers his war counsel together, I shall send forth my immortal army to set the stage for the *real* war."

High above time and space, King Elyon, alerted to Asmo's plot summoned Prince Sabaoth to ready the celestial warriors. The time had come for the immortal spirits to fight side by side with the mortals who loved their invisible King.

Lord Perazim brought warnings through dreams in the night to King Waymon and Bishop Bryan. Christiana woke in the wee hours with a heaviness of impending doom. Others through-out Brighton Castle and the realm of Britanniae, including Bane Manor, began to call upon King

Elyon to help them. *"Help them from what?"* They did not know.

Preparing for War

As the hazy sun slowly rose through the low misty clouds, pockets of fog drifted lazily across the wide plain. Birds noisily chirped somewhere off in the distance filling the air with song. The inhabitants of Brighton Castle awoke to the dawning of a new day full of promise.

As the massive drawbridge lowered for the day, the gatekeeper spied fast approaching riders bearing a foreign insignia on their flag.

"We must zee your king," breathlessly said one of the messengers in a foreign accent. "Eet eze most urgent."

The gatekeeper called for a guard to escort the foreigners to the palace. Arriving at the imposing structure, the messengers dismounted and ascended the steps where a sentry stood erect at attention. "We bring urgent news for zee king," one said.

"The king is only just rising," protested the sentry.

"Theze cannot wait," said the messenger.

"I will inform his majesty's chamberlain," came the reply.

King Waymon received the messengers with all grace. "What is so urgent that protocol is abandoned?"

"I bring a message from the Emperor of Valois," the messenger said. Breaking the seal, the messenger unrolled the scroll and read:

"This is what the Great and Powerful Emperor of Valois declares:

"You boast of military strength - but you speak only empty words. On whom are you depending? If you say to me 'We depend on King Elyon the Most High,' I tell you that King Elyon told me himself to march against this country and destroy it. I have already conquered all the regions surrounding my nation. Your High King did not save any of them. I will lay waste your kingdom, as well."

The messenger rerolled the scroll, handed it to the king and departed.

King Waymon's face turned ashen as he took the scroll and went straight to the cathedral. He walked all the way to the front and laid prostrate before the altar. Unrolling the scroll, the king cried out,

"O Lord, Ruler of Britanniae, enthroned between the cherubim, you alone are Sovereign over all the kingdoms of the earth. You have made the celestial city and earth. Give ear, O Most High, and hear; open your eyes, O Lord and see; listen to the words Emperor Beaudonnier has sent to insult the living King.

"It is true, O Lord, that the Valis'ion armies have laid waste these nations and their lands. They have thrown their gods into the fire and destroyed them, for they were not gods but only wood and stone, fashioned by men's hands. Now, O Lord our Sovereign, deliver us from his hand, so that all the kingdoms on earth may know that you alone, O Lord, are Ruler."

The king called for his war counsel along with Bishop Bryan. "Valois is attacking us," he said.

"Our first order of business is to call upon King Elyon.," said the Bishop, "We must implore our Great Sovereign to send his celestial warriors to help us in this mortal battle. There will be no victory if we do not call upon His name."

Bishop Bryan summoned all the inhabitants of Brighton Castle to assemble in the courtyard. The minstrels brought their instruments and banners. King Waymon read the message aloud to the assembly. Then the trumpeters raised their instruments beginning a song that would ascend into the eternal realm of King Elyon. The rest of the minstrels played their instruments as the singers joined their voices together. Sekiah followed Lady Elizabeth as she led the worship warriors waiving banners like a backdrop to Garrett and the other war dancers moving in step to the rhythm of the song.

When the musical plea ended, King Waymon met with the high constable, Sir Graham. Sir Graham gave orders for the field marshal and the commander of the garrison to ready the troops and gear up the armory with as much additional weaponry as possible.

Sir John, the field marshal, summoned Garrett and Sekiah and two of his own squires. "I need all my knights here, so I must send you forth to alert the neighboring castles and rally more forces," he said, handing each one scrolls with the king's seal to deliver.

"Sekiah," stated the field marshal, "take the same route back to Bane Manor that you used in coming here. However, I want you to bypass Brookshire."

Sekiah felt a rush of relief that he would not have to face the peasants there alone.

"Garrett, I am sending you to Duke James of Gilbert on the west side of Brighton Castle. From there you will ride through the village of Esyngwald on your way back to Bane Manor.

As Sekiah prepared to depart, Sir Spencer came over to him. "Sekiah," he said, handing the squire a rolled up piece of parchment. "I have a note for you to give Devynne."

Taking it, Sekiah replied, "I will make sure she receives it, sir." Then he unlatched his saddlebag to put the note inside.

Sir Spencer looked intently at his young squire before him. But not knowing what to say, simply said with deep feeling, "God speed."
Sir Tyler wished Garrett the same. "We do not know when we shall meet again," Sir Tyler said. "You are traveling a new route and alone this time.

"Not quite sir," responded the squire. "I have the celestial warriors going before me."

"That you have!" smiled the knight. "All the same, take care until you reach Bane Manor again."

"Thank you, sir," Garrett said as he nudged Valiant to trot toward the castle gate and across the drawbridge. Garrett and Sekiah rode out together until the road split in opposite directions.

"Meet you back at the manor!" Sekiah waved.

"I'll be waiting!" hollered Garrett leaning into Valiant to gallop off.

Skirmishes

Chapter 19

"**I** need scouts to gather information to bring back to us," said Sir John. "I will also be sending archers to harass the enemy as they come ashore. That will slow them down and buy us time for the reinforcements to arrive."

"Sir Spencer, you will be in charge of the skirmish," said Sir John. "Your new rank is Lieutenant since you are now in charge of a platoon."

The young knight looked astonished at the field marshal.

"I know you have just been knighted," reassured the officer. "I also know that you are up to the task."

"Thank you sir," Sir Spencer replied.

Lt. Spencer took the scouts and archers. The party rode through the afternoon arriving at Brookshire as the sun began its decent beyond the horizon. Sheriff Festus anxiously approached Lieutenant Spencer. However, before he could speak the young lieutenant dismounted and handed him the notice from the king.

With trepidation that he might receive a reprimand from the king for the incident a few days prior with the soldiers and Christiana, the sheriff read the notice. The initial relief that the message did not concern that matter instantly vanished with the more worrisome news of a major attack upon Britanniae! Not only that, but the invader's course took them right through Brookshire! The town's only safety meant fleeing to the protection of Brighton Castle.

Sheriff Festus called the town together. Sir Spencer addressed the gathered peasants. "The Valis'ion' are on their way to attack Brighton Castle. We are going to Fregee'–by-the-Water to hinder their advancement. You must take your livestock and flee to the castle."

By midday the peasants of Brookshire crossed the open plain to the castle joining together with the inhabitants of other surrounding villages bringing with them their tools, livestock and whatever provisions they could.

The teeming mass of peasants and serfs pouring through the gates quickly filled the courtyard. The lord mayor and his officers worked to minimize the confusion by establishing order and helping the families get settled. King Waymon through an edict given to the lord mayor enlisted the employ of all the peasants during the siege.

Lt. Spencer and his scouts arrived at the port city of Fregee'-on-the-Water where the Valis'ion' army disembarked. Their position high above the sandy beach gave the soldiers sufficient advantage.

"Those Valois ships are large and numerous," said an archer in awe.

"They are a force to be reckoned with, that is for sure," said Lt. Spencer.

Watching as the enemy unloaded their mass weapons of warfare, the scouts devised their plan.

Lt. Spencer sent a squire back to Brighton Castle to tell Sir Graham what kind of forces advanced toward the castle and to relate his plans. Lt. Spencer speculated that without interference, it would take the army approximately a fortnight to unload all the ships and a month, perhaps two, to begin the siege on Brighton Castle. The enemy appeared to be 16,000 troops and 13,000 horses strong. However, the young lieutenant had a plan to delay the movement of the enemy.

Under cover of the deserted town above the docks, Lt. Spencer sent his archers to various spots overlooking the enemy vessels. After igniting their fire pot, each archer lit his arrow and sent it flaming toward the soldiers keeping watch. Thus began the unrelenting hailstorm of flaming arrows pelting the dock, the guards and supply ships. As arrows found their mark, sentries hit the sand with their tunics going up in flames. Momentary panic stopped the unloading of the siege weapons. The dock caught fire and the mast went up in flames as well as the hull of the ship carrying the Emperor with his retinue. Soldiers quickly found buckets and any other item they could to douse the flames.

The emperor, hastily fleeing his ship into another boat raged against his nemesis. "Just wait teell you taste my wrath against you, King Waymon!"

The Valis'ion retaliated with their own barrage of brightly lit arrows shooting past the scouts. The torrent of missiles volleyed in all directions. Into the twilight of the dawn, arrows flew between the scouts and the Valois. Through the onslaught of arrows the Valis'ion continued to unload their weapons.

With the firefight igniting numerous buildings and daylight fast approaching, Lt. Spencer along with his archers made a rapid retreat back to Brighton Castle.

In their war counsel, Lt. Spencer recounted the skirmish at the port. Sir Graham and the other warriors of the counsel strategized ways to further impede the advancing army.

"Well done!" Sir Graham said addressing Lt. Spencer. "I had confidence in you and you met my expectation."

"Thank you, Sir," replied Lt. Spencer.

"I will need you here now to help with the incoming soldiers and their squires. You will also be working with Sir Tyler, who also has been given the rank of Lieutenant. "

"Yes sir," answered Lt. Spencer, feeling a sense of anticipation at seeing Sir Roderick and many other knights again that he knew.

Sir Graham ordered another of his high officers to establish a forward camp on the cliffs above the port. Over the course of the next several days, the tactical squads and company of archers hindered the progression of the Valois. One squad lobbed boulders from the rocky cliff above onto the marching army while the other squad shot arrows.

A messenger arrived to the forward camp. Handing the officer the order from Sir Graham, he read,

"Reinforcements arrived. Begin the retreat to Brighton Castle."

In the course of their fall back, the officer positioned his squads to continue causing confusion to the advancing army by their quick assailments.

Emperor Beaudonnier became frustrated at the delay caused by the Britaniaens. Relentlessly forcing his officers to push their troops on through the continuous attack, the emperor yelled at his commanders. "You are cowards! Where are your guts?!"

"Lying on zee ground," the general muttered under his breath.

"Zeze leettle nation humiliated us when we fought against zem before," railed the emperor. "For zee glory of Valois we shall triumph! We weel show zee world zat Valois eze NOT to be trifled weeth."

"We zuffer heavy losses already," complained the commander. "We have not even reached zee castle and zee troops grow discouraged."

"Eef you weesh to remain my general, zen you must use your resourcefulness to gain zee upper hand!" screamed Emperor Beaudonnier.

At last the squads relented as they high-tailed it back the final leg to the castle. Now the Valois could press forward unimpeded.

Attacked!

Staging

Chapter 20

The sound of pounding hoofs thundering across the drawbridge reverberated throughout the castle. The soldiers arriving ahead of the siege filled the inhabitants with awe. The multitudes of knights and mortals-at-arms including the yeomen, who left their farms with their weapons, came from all over Britanniae.

Sir Graham masterfully oversaw the assembly of incoming soldiers. He grouped the soldiers into armies, counted by lances. Each lance was made up of one knight plus five other squires and yeomen. The garrison also included many archers and foot soldiers.

Lieutenants Spencer and Tyler worked together under Sir Graham.

"Have you seen Sir Roderick or anyone from Bane Manor?" Lt. Tyler asked his friend.

"I have not even seen Sir Leo or any of his soldiers," replied Lt. Spencer, frowning.

"What perchance has become of our squires?" Lt. Tyler asked with grave concern.

Sir John, who had now returned from the skirmishes, oversaw the erection and positioning of the trebuchets and mangonels on the battements.

William of Fregee' oversaw the bucket brigade. He instructed the civilians on procedures for maintaining the water supplies around the castle during the fiery assault.

Amidst the frightened peasants from the king's land fleeing into the safety of the castle, walked a woman carrying a staff. Her erect posture and rod projected an air of poise and confidence.

Upon observing the woman who stood out from among the rest, a curious lad approached her.

"Might I ask you a question?" inquired the youth.

"And who art thou?" asked the woman.

"I am Kynton, son of Hubert," answered the lad.

"I am Morfydd," replied the woman. "What doth thou wish to know?"

"How is it that you walk without fear?" Kynton asked. "Even my father worries about the war and he is a brave yeoman."

"I believe in the power of the super-natural," answered Morfydd.

"Yes," replied Kynton, "the celestial warriors are on our side!"

"Where is your family?" asked the woman.

"My father has gone to the castle already. My mother tends to the younger children," answered the lad. "My sister helps her. I just stay out of the way."

"That is helpful in its own way," stated Morfydd. "Perchance I could school you in the ways of confidence and fortitude."

With that aim welling up in the innocent lad's heart, Kynton walked straighter and lighter already.

Bishop Bryan supervised the preparation of the infirmary for the advent of many casualties. Christiana and Blind Jessie assisted Ladies Elizabeth and Suzanne to make ready the infirmary.

"My name is Morfydd," the stately peasant woman said, coming into the building where the women worked. "My young friend Kynton and I would like to be of service to you."

"Thank you," replied Lady Suzanne. "Christiana can show you what needs to be done."

The Valois positioned their encampments at a safe distance from the castle's long-range catapults and crossbows. They built palisade fences for their own protection. The Emperor sent out troops to cut off as many points of access to the castle as possible. The troops worked feverishly many days assembling and positioning the powerful siege weapons. They constructed the mighty trebuchet, catapults, mangonels, battering rams, siege towers and ballistae.

At night scores of campfires glowed brightly up through the trees. Emperor Beaudonnier gloated to his officers that the sight of the numerous campfires would cause the inhabitants of the castle to tremble.

Asmo watched the Valois encampment from above. He assigned his asmode war commander, Rofocale, to advise Emperor Beaudonnier.

"Ze longer we take making sure everything eez ready," Rofocale slobbered in the emperor's ear, *"zee better prepared Brighton Castle weell be to withstand ze siege."*

"But ze siege engines are not ready yet," the emperor thought, believing he reasoned with himself.

"*King Waymon's reports tell heem zat we are not ready for another fortnight,*" Rofocale slobbered again.

"Yes," Emperor Beaudonnier agreed. "*Brighton Castle may not be as difficult to take eef we start our warfare now.*

Consulting with his war counsel Emperor Beaudonnier decided to attack at dawn.

"We estimate another two weeks to position all our siege engines," protested the general.

"King Waymon knows zat," answered the emperor. "Zat eez why we must catch zem off-guard. Zey are steell waiting large troops that have not come."

"Zat is true," replied a general. "Eet eez better to take ze lead even though we may not be completely ready ourselves zan to finish and have ze rest of zeir army in force."

King Waymon could not sleep. He paced the floor in his chambers. Sometime in the night a large celestial warrior came to his room.

"Do not be afraid," the celestial warrior said, observing the king's astonished countenance. "I have come in the name of King Elyon to tell you that though you must fight this great battle, he has sent us to aide you. Emperor Beaudonnier is working this night to attack at first light. I will give you King Elyon's strategy, but now you must rouse the garrison."

The king called for his high constable, Sir Graham. "Emperor Beaudonnier is planning to attack at dawn. We must be in position before then."

Sir Graham woke the garrison. All mortals-at-arms reached their stations on the battlements and towers.

Ladies Elizabeth and Suzanne rose and gathered the spiritual warriors together in the great cathedral.

"Come, Lord Perazim!" invoked Lady Elizabeth. "Cover us with your cloud of protection from the spies and weapons of the enemy. Direct the arrows and the artillery of our soldiers to hit their marks. Minimize casualties and shorten the length of this siege."

Other voices ascended in petition to King Elyon.

Warfare

In the predawn light, the Valis'ion army emerged out from among the trees and poured onto the expansive plain. As the attackers crossed the field, arrows and large stones propelled from catapults suddenly filled the sky. Archers shot their crossbows from small, slit-shaped windows in the castle walls or between the battlements. Foot soldiers fell to the ground as others by-passed them in their mission to reach the castle. Still other archers returned fire.

Emperor Beaudonnier raged at his foiled plot to catch Brighton Castle off guard. "Eef zey were prepared for our surprise attack," the emperor ranted, "what else do zey know; and more importantly, *how* do zey know?!

Rofocale flew up to Asmo to inform him of the turn of events.

"Prince Sabaoth has his spies about the Valis'ion camp," Asmo mused, more to himself than to Rofocale. Then with cunning in his fiery eyes and steam smoldering from his mouth, Asmo ordered, "Find out what is going on at the castle and see how to infiltrate it. Surely not all the inhabitants are loyal subjects of King Waymon. What we need is a mortal willing to commit treason. Take Egon and Duplicity with you," ordered Asmo.

The Valis'ion troops rolled the battering rams and siege towers toward Brighton Castle. As they came into close proximity of the main gate and tower, Sir John readied his armies.

"Fire the catapult!" yelled Sir John.

Flaming arrows shot toward the wooden battering ram and siege towers to set them on fire as the attackers pushed the massive structures toward the castle wall. The siege tower protected the advancing soldiers and also enabled them to raise ladders inside it for climbing the castle wall.

Lt. Tyler and his detachment in the tower of the outermost curtain wall fought to repel the onslaught of the Valois.

The flaming bucket of oil slammed into the opening of the siege tower setting it on fire and spilling down on the troops climbing up the ladder. Lt. Tyler succeeded in thwarting the attack on the tower.

The lieutenant now turned his attention toward the fast approaching enemy archers.

"Ready the catapult. At my signal fire the volley!" cried the Lieutenant. "Ready, FIRE! Reload. Ready, FIRE!"

The initial archer's assault of the Valis'ion failed with many casualties, causing a hasty retreat.

Rofocale, along with his underlings flew toward Brighton Castle. The asmodai could easily see where the strength lay within its walls: A cloud of protection covered the castle.

"I see a small clearing in the cloud," Egon pointed out to Rofocale. "The aroma wafting through it summons help from Asmo."

"Yes," the asmode commander affirmed. "Let us investigate the source of the gap."

Swooping through the opening, the asmodai hovered close to the witch, Morfydd, secretly practicing the ancient craft of sorcery. Kneeling in the midst of ritual they watched as she used her potions for conjuring to destroy Brighton Castle.

"We have found our ally and tool for treachery," Rofocale said with glee. "While the Valis'ion army destroys brick and mortar, we shall use this sorceress to bring down the castle from within," Rofocale said with jubilant smugness.

"Egon, stay close to Morfydd and respond to her bidding." We shall return to Asmo and inform him of our discovery."

"Be sure to tell him that I am the one who found the opening," Egon said as Rofocale and Duplicity flew off. "I will not get credit for my work," the grotesque little asmode sniveled petulantly.

As Rofocale darted his way through the opening, he spotted another breach in the protective mist.

"What is this?" The asmode said with great interest. "Another ally," Rofocale stated upon recognizing Petronilla. "Only this one will not abide Morfydd because she does not know that they are actually on the same side. Duplicity, instruct Petronilla on the sly ways of causing division without being discovered," Rofocale commanded as he winged his way back to Asmo with the important news of his finds.

Days of warfare turned into weeks. At first, Brighton Castle kept the upper hand in the siege. However, over the course of time, the relentless pounding of the battering rams took their toll on the fortress. The metal head fitted onto the huge tree trunks shook, pounded and battered the castle wall and gate.

The king's war counsel met.

"How long before they breech the outer curtain wall?" asked King Waymon.

"It appears imminent, Your Majesty," answered Sir Graham."

"We must call a fast," said Bishop Bryan. "There is a reason Valois is gaining the upper hand. We need to hear from King Elyon. We must separate ourselves from everything that instills fear and brings confusion. We cannot allow anything to undermine our peace and stability in King Elyon. If we do this, we will be able to see clearly the attack of the enemy against us, which will then position us to resist him while we maintain spiritual integrity. King Elyon will give us this insight if set our hearts to see."

"Where are the celestial warriors King Elyon promised?" asked Sir Graham.

"If Your Majesty pleases," interjected Sir John, "the soldiers cannot fast while they are fighting."

"That is true," answered the king. "We will call all civilians to fast for three days."

On the backside of Brighton Castle, the army did not fare well. The Valis'ion's trebuchet penetrated the castle's first curtain wall. The captain and his detachment fell, utterly annihilated.

Sir John gave the order for all the armies to fall back to the second curtain wall. During the retreat, Lt. Spencer and his army encountered vicious hand-to-hand combat with broadswords, spears and double-bladed battleaxes.

"Prince Sabaoth!" Lt. Spencer loudly called, "Send your celestial warriors!" Sustaining some casualties, Lt. Spencer and his detachment reached the second curtain wall.

"Here are more cloths for you to make bandages with," said Blind Jessie. "When your stack is full, take them over to the infirmary."

Morfydd took out a vial she carried with her in her pouch and smeared a dab on her finger. The sorceress touched each sheet as she ripped it into strips. Under her breath, Morfydd placed a hex for disease and death upon the cloths.

Jessie perceived the tone of the atmosphere in the room change to become cold and chilling. She sensed the presence of the asmodai and began to whisper to King Elyon in her secret language.

Morfydd however, did not notice that Blind Jessie had detected her clandestine actions.

"Kynton, take Jessie's bundle and come with me to the infirmary," the sorceress said, gathering her strips into a large bundle. Carefully they made their way to the nearby infirmary, avoiding the incoming arrows and other projectiles.

When Blind Jessie knew that Morfydd had left, she asked Lady Suzanne, "Did you happen to observe what Morfydd was doing with the cloths?"

"My back was turned," Lady Suzanne answered. "However, I did note the presence of evil."

"What should we do now?" asked Blind Jessie. "I think she is a traitor and schemes to kill our wounded. I believe that Lord Perazim is revealing to me that Morfydd placed a hex on the sheets of cloth."

"Yes," agreed Lady Suzanne. "I feel that I must tell the bishop."

"Be careful!" Jessie said earnestly.

Lady Suzanne opened the door and sped away, staying close to the buildings.

A fireball landed just outside the cloth shop next to the infirmary. As the water brigade attacked the fire, William of Fregee' entered the infirmary.

"We must evacuate the infirmary," he said as he and another from the brigade began to help move some of the wounded.

"Blind Jessie and Lady Susanne are in the cloth shop!" gasped Christiana.

"I will get them out," said William, running to the door as he beckoned a couple of strong mortals from the brigade to help.

Coming out of the infirmary, William struggled to make his way around the blazing fire without being hit by any projectiles.

"Jessie, Lady Suzanne!" he hollered.

"I am here!" Jessie yelled back. "Lady Suzanne has gone to see the bishop. What is happening?"

"A fireball landed close by and I need to get you out. Do not be afraid," William said in a reassuring voice.

"I am all right," Jessie replied. "Warfare is frightening, but Lord Perazim gave peace to me," the maiden said with confidence.

Victories occurred, but setbacks became commonplace. The moral inside Brighton Castle diminished. Peasants and soldiers alike felt greatly discouraged. Where were the celestial warriors?

Asmo watched the siege with great interest. "Mortals killing each other; how entertaining!" He said gleefully to Rofocale.

"King Elyon made these foolish mortals in His own image," replied Rofocale.

"That was His great mistake," Asmo said with satisfaction. "Each time a mortal dies it is like destroying a part of King Elyon. My army is accomplishing my goal by directing the Valis'ion commanders. Emperor Beaudonnier, my pawn, is bringing down that proud citadel. At long last I, Asmo, the greatest celestial being have the upper hand!"

Captured!

Chapter 21

Garrett rode as hard as Valiant could go. The young squire fought against fear as he sat long hours in the saddle. The lad found it difficult to focus on anything other than the siege about to overcome beautiful Brighton Castle and its inhabitants. If King Waymon lost, then all of Britanniae would become the subjects of the detestable Emperor Beaudonnier.

"Will we be forced to learn a new language, too?" Garrett said aloud to no one, but himself. "We *cannot* lose!"

The heat of the bright noonday sun beating down upon the earth caused Valiant to slow his pace and Garrett to become weary in the saddle. Eventually the young soldier dismounted. Valiant grazed in the meadow while the hungry young soldier devoured his lunch. Sir John had made certain that the saddle bags of all the squires sent out were filled with plenty of victuals for the first leg of their journey. Soon the young messenger mounted-up and continued on his way again.

The afternoon ride found Garrett in another frame of mind. Instead of fear and anxiety, the squire determined to focus his imagination on the invisible realm where the real battle for Brighton Castle raged. The young warrior visualized the celestial warriors brandishing their swords as they slew the evil asmodai causing the Valis'ion army to suffer many setbacks and heavy losses. Taking heart by the images in his mind, Garrett began to sing songs of victory and praise. Valiant felt the change come over his rider and quickened his pace a bit.

Finally the sun began its decent. Horse and rider covered much ground the first day. Feeling too weary to continue any further, he dismounted and spent the night under the stars.

As daybreak overtook the darkness, Garrett woke almost more exhausted from lying on the cold hard ground. His thin blanket did not provide adequate warmth, either. The youth's stomach growled ferociously. Eagerly taking out the ration for his breakfast, Garrett wolfed down the now stale bread and hunk of hard cheese. Then he gulped several large swigs of water before mounting up again. Once more, horse and rider continued on for another full day.

Garrett encouraged himself again as he sat in the saddle. When he tired of singing, the young soldier entertained himself by picturing the celestial warfare taking place. Garrett knew that the outcome greatly depended on the faith and prayers of the mortals; so he cried out to King Elyon to strengthen the fortitude and faith of the troops and civilians.

"Help the worship warriors to fight with their songs and proclamations. Help King Waymon to make wise strategic decisions. Help Sir John and Sir Graham to lead the armies as they and the soldiers protect the castle and its inhabitants."

When he could no longer think of words to say, Garrett used the secret language to petition the war counsel in heaven. That brought a humorous scene to his mind as the squire visualized the asmodai trying to decipher his words before they reached the throne room. The confusion that the secret messages caused as they passed through enemy lines in the heavenlies made Garrett laugh out loud!

Toward dusk, Garrett spied Gilbert Manor, a very modern looking castle. Gothic - not at all like the Edwardian style. The tall structure surrounded by a wide moat silhouetted against the changing hues of the evening sky, made a picturesque setting. Sensing they could make it before nightfall, Valiant quickened his pace. Horse and rider arrived just before the raising of the drawbridge.

"I bring urgent news for Duke James of Gilbert," Garrett announced to the gatekeeper."

Raising the gate, the cordial keeper replied, "I shall take ye to him me self."

Garrett dismounted and passed his reins off to a stable boy.

The gatekeeper pulled on the cord to ring the bell of the manor house. In a few moments a dignified servant answered.

"This here squire comes with urgent news for the duke," the gatekeeper informed the servant. Then he turned and departed.

"I shall notify His Grace," responded the servant. "Wait in here," the servant said as he ushered Garrett into the hallway.

Soon, a finely dressed noble appeared. In a warm and friendly manner the gentleman introduced himself. "I am Duke James. My servant tells me you come with important information."

"Yes, Your Grace," answered Garrett, handing the duke the scroll from King Waymon.

Untying the scroll and unrolling the parchment, the duke read the king's edict to join forces. "We are at war," stated the duke to himself. Turning to the servant he instructed, "Take this squire to the kitchen for some supper and he shall rest the night with us."

Addressing Garrett, the duke asked, "By the way, what is your name and where is your next destination?"

"I am Garrett. Tomorrow I go through Esyngwald on my way back to Bane Manor, to Sir Roderick, my liege lord," stated Garrett.

"You have traveled quite extensively," said the duke. "The next two days will be long ones in the saddle again. In the morning, I will be sure to have cook fill your saddle bags. I am certain you have eaten the good rations from the castle by now! I will also have a message ready for you to deliver to Sir Roderick. I can see how tired you are. We will talk in the morning before you journey on," Duke James said as they parted for the night.

That night, Garrett slept deeply. In the morning he awoke ready to meet the day. The lad enjoyed a hearty breakfast with the duke and his family.

"Tell us about Brighton Castle," asked the duke's son, Jacob. "Is it as grand as they say?"

"It is even grander than any description can give account. It is the fairest of all castles and immense in size!" Garrett said as he relived his first impression. "The castle is a complete containment of all necessities within its walls. There are outer walls, to be sure, and inner walls, as well. "

"What is the king himself like?" asked Joy.

"Children," reproved the duchess, "we have told you many stories of Brighton Castle and the king."

"But mamma," implored Joy downcast. "We want to hear all about it from someone who has just been there."

"I do not mind telling about my impressions at all," Garrett interjected.

"Go on, please," said Duchess Karen.

Continuing, Garrett said with a smile. "The king is not what one might expect from a royal sovereign."

"Is he not regal, then?" questioned Jacob.

"Ah," replied the squire. "The king is certainly regal, but he is also a warrior king who has seen many battles in his day. He is humble and devoted to the Sovereign of all sovereigns. That is what I mean. There is no haughtiness to be found in him. He has a grand sense of humour, too. The king makes all those in his company to be at ease, yet he also has a commanding presence that inspires respect."

"The children are very excited about the jousting tournament the king is holding," said the duke. "My garrison is preparing for the competitions."

Ushering the children to their morning lessons, the duke said to Garrett, "Tell me about the battle ensuing. With war unfolding, plans are subject to change. How is it that you travel alone from the castle, yet you hail from Bane Manor?"

"Two of the king's heralds were waylaid on their way to Bane Manor a fortnight ago," said Garrett. "They were overcome by a band of Vikings. The one we found during a hunting expedition had been left for dead, but the other was taken prisoner. Lord Roderick dispatched two of his errant knights and their squires to inform King Waymon. It was while we were at Brighton Castle that Emperor Beaudonnier began preparations for the siege. King Waymon sent several squires throughout Britanniae to rally the forces. The Valis'ion army is even now surrounding Brighton Castle," Garrett said gravely. "Their weapons are many and massive."

"When I and my knights meet up with Sir Leo and Sir Roderick with their soldiers, we will strategize together as to how to approach the enemy with our armies," stated the duke.

"In the meantime," said Duke James, "you must be off so that you will reach your next destination by supper. Give my greetings to Sheriff Dan. He does a fine job of overseeing the town of Esyngwald and surrounding villages."

With his saddlebags filled again with victuals for the day's journey ahead, Garrett set out on Valiant with a joyful heart, knowing his journey neared its end.

"God speed!" waived the duke as Garret rode away.

This day, Garrett's thoughts turned toward Bane Manor. Anticipation filled his heart knowing that by the morrow his long journey, full of adventures, would at last be ended. He wondered if Sekiah had arrived first to greet him or himself still plodding over hill and dale. The joyful songs from Brighton Castle repeated themselves in his heart until they found their way into Garrett's voice. Feeling uninhibited, he sang with abandon.

"I am a warrior, a war dancer for my king
It is to King Elyon that I love to sing.
He alone gives me Faith to fight
I fight for mortals with supernatural might
So all will dance and sing unto our Good
and Great King."

The squire at last arrived in Esyngwald. The rosy glow of the late afternoon sun cast a soft light over the small cluster of hovels and buildings making up the rural community.

"Greetings, young soldier," the burly sheriff said as he looked up from his work in the stable. Walking over to Garrett to welcome him, the gregarious town official introduced himself. "I am Sheriff Dan."

"I am Squire Garrett of Bane Manor," said Garrett. "Duke James sends his greetings."

"This is my daughter Tori," the sheriff said as the young inquisitive girl came up to them. "What brings thee to our humble village?" Sheriff Dan inquired.

"I seek lodging for the night." Dismounting, the squire continued, "I am passing through on my return from Brighton Castle. I am sent by King Waymon to rally the soldiers for war," replied Garrett.

"What trouble comes our way?" asked Sheriff Dan, furrowing his brow in concern.

"Valois has invaded Britanniae and set a siege against Brighton Castle," answered Garrett.

"That is disturbing news," Sheriff Dan said with heaviness in his voice.

"Will we be attacked too, papa?" the child asked.

"Brighton Castle is far from here," her father answered reassuringly.

Then the sheriff said warmly to Garrett, "Follow me to the stables where you may water and feed your noble steed."

"I will draw the bucket of water from the well for you!" Tori said excitedly. "What is your horse's name?" she asked.

"Valiant," said the lad.

"Valiant," Tori said to the steed, "I will take care of you. You are a noble horse." She softly patted his cheek as he nuzzled her neck.

Seeing that Valiant was tended to, Garrett mentioned his own hunger.

"Come," invited the sheriff, "our dwellings are modest, but you are heartily welcome," he said as he led the young lad toward his own hovel.

"I am spent from my long journey and am grateful for your generosity," replied the squire.

"Sherrie," Sheriff Dan called to his wife. "I have brought a soldier home to dine with us," he announced.

The sheriff and his family showed gracious hospitality toward Garrett.

Sitting down to supper, the sheriff remarked to Garrett, "Do not mind the flirtations of my young daughter; Tori has never met a soldier before, and I am afraid she is smitten."

Tori blushed as she set the plate of rolls on the table next to Garrett.

"She is quite pretty," remarked Garrett. "How old is your daughter?"

"Tori nears the end of childhood," the sheriff answered. "In just a few years it will be time to find her a husband."

"Tell us about Brighton Castle and the king," said the Sheriff.

"We peasant folk can only wonder what life in such a grand place must be like," commented Sherrie.

"Is the queen as beautiful as the Duchess Karen?" asked Tori.

"Yes," answered Garrett, as he proceeded to describe for them his memories and impressions of his visit there.

When the evening drew to a close, Tori took Garrett upstairs to the loft where he would sleep. Leaving the candle on a small table, the girl quickly said, "Goodnight," and retreated down the stairs.

Turning in for the night, Garrett blew the candle out and lay down on the straw bed. *"This time tomorrow,"* Garrett thought to himself, *"I will once again lie in my own bed!"* The weary soldier drifted off to sleep thinking about life at Bane Manor.

The moonless night full of stars blanketed the village in quiet calm as the inhabitants of Esyngwald slept in peaceful slumber.

Under the heavy cloak of darkness, only the splash of oars broke the stillness of the night giving indication of approaching boats. The shallow longships with broad bottoms allowed the vessels to land on any sandy beach, including places where a raid was believed unthinkable.

Prisoners from recent raids sat in chains as they manned the oars. Heavy sorrow engulfed the captives who waited helplessly while their captors went ashore.

The herald's blistered wrists and ankles seeped from the chafing caused by the shackles. His back ached and his arms felt weary from rowing. Cole's real agony, however, lay in his heart for the poor innocents who would soon be taken away along with him to a far distant land, never to return. For the thousandth time, the herald wondered what had become of his friend and companion, Cedric. *"Oh King Elyon,"* the mortal silently cried, *"did these pagan heathens kill Cedric? "Tis better that than to suffer my fate – never knowing and never being free."*

Alighting from their vessels, the dozen or so attackers stealthily ran up the sandy beach and into the small village where they caught the sleeping inhabitants unaware.

Without warning, shrieks of terror shattered the tranquility of sleep. Sheriff Dan rushed into the street to discover the cause of such alarm. Garrett bolted upright in his bed. Working to make sense of the nightmare, he hurriedly dressed himself as embers began to fall around.

Dashing down the stairs Garrett heard the panicked cries of Sherrie and Tori. Looking through the open doorway, the young soldier could see silhouettes running helter skelter as flaming torches flew upward catching thatched roofs on fire.

Suddenly the figure of a fearsome warrior, dressed in leather hides and strange helmet engulfed the doorway. Garrett's mind reeled. *"These are not Valis'ion,"* he realized. *"These are Vikings!"*

Sherrie loudly gasped as she reached for Tori. Tori, however, leapt through the nearby open window. Landing in the garden behind the house, the child scrambled up and escaped through the mayhem and fled into the woods.

Garrett tried to protect Sherrie, but the fierce Viking easily overpowered the youth by knocking him down with his shield. Sherrie stood helplessly quivering against the wall, tears streaming down her face.

Next, the warrior dragged them both out into the street to be shackled with the other prisoners from Esyngwald. The street, brightly lit as if by one huge bonfire revealed the bedlam before them. The scene of destruction along with the piercing sounds of crying and screaming engulfed their senses.

Through the smoke in the distance, Garrett thought he could see and hear Valiant and some other horses loudly snort as they raced out of the burning stable.

Garrett struggled against the fetters until one of the Vikings forcefully struck him across the shoulders with the broadside of his sword. Garrett fell from the severe blow. One of the Vikings pulled Garrett to his feet. Rising, he spied the sheriff lying on the ground. *"Was he dead?"* Garrett wondered. He dared not let Sherrie see him. He shuffled with the distraught villagers to the beach where the Viking's longships waited to take them away. Sherrie wept while she frantically wailed for Tori and Dan.

"King Elyon!" Garrett yelled at the top of his lungs. "Where are you? Prince Sabaoth! Where are the celestial warriors?! Are they all at the castle? How can this be happening to me? I had my armour on....!"

www.ingramcontent.com/pod-product-compliance
Lightning Source LLC
Chambersburg PA
CBHW070340260626
47160CB00003B/1097